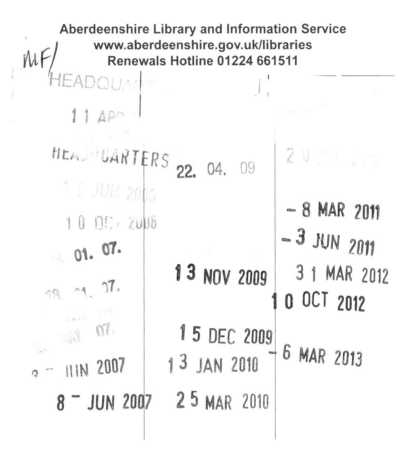

MF/

HEADQUA

11 AP

HEA. QARTERS 22. 04. 09   2 U

1 5 JUN 20

1 0 OC. 2008

01. 07.

18. 01. 07.

MAY 07

2 - IIIN 2007

8 - JUN 2007

13 NOV 2009

15 DEC 2009

13 JAN 2010

25 MAR 2010

- 8 MAR 2011

- 3 JUN 2011

3 1 MAR 2012

1 0 OCT 2012

- 6 MAR 2013

FORREST, Richard

Death at King Arthur's
Court

DEATH AT KING ARTHUR'S COURT

DEATH AT KING ARTHUR'S COURT

A Lyon and Bea Wentworth Mystery

Richard Forrest

severn
House

This first world edition published in Great Britain 2005 by
SEVERN HOUSE PUBLISHERS LTD of
9–15 High Street, Sutton, Surrey SM1 1DF.
This first world edition published in the USA 2006 by
SEVERN HOUSE PUBLISHERS INC of
595 Madison Avenue, New York, N.Y. 10022.

British Library Cataloguing in Publication Data

Forrest, Richard, 1932-
    Death at King Arthur's Court. - (The Lyon and Bea Wentworth adventures)
    1.   Wentworth, Lyon (Fictitious character) - Fiction
    2.   Wentworth, Bea (Fictitious character) - Fiction
    3.   Authors, American - Connecticut - Fiction
    4.   Women legislators - Connecticut - Fiction
    5.   Detective and mystery stories
    I.   Title
    813.5'4 [F]

    ISBN-10 : 0-7278-6314-2

Typeset by Palimpsest Book Production Ltd.,
Polmont, Stirlingshire, Scotland.
Printed and bound in Great Britain by
MPG Books Ltd., Bodmin, Cornwall.

To the next generation – Cassie, Mia, Atticus, Eliza, Alex, Kate, Sasha, Max, Caitlin, Freia, Jane, Jack, Sebastian, Dylan, and Gabrielle.

One

The sword swept through the air and bit into a tree trunk inches from Lyon Wentworth's head.

A five-inch wood chip spun away as it was carved from the pine. The sword twisted free and was slowly raised for another thrust. The blade shifted for a vertical blow with enough force to nearly cut him in half.

He threw himself to the side and stumbled backward over a moss-covered boulder. The sword's downward arc followed his fall. Metal and rock clashed with a clang that echoed through the misty woods.

He lurched to his feet to stumble forward. His breath came in rasping gulps. He ran in a weaving pattern toward the edge of the high promontory a hundred feet above the Connecticut River. He was confused. His vision was faulty, and his legs were leaden and unresponsive. His pursuer moved slowly but persistently forward. It was impossible not to glance back. The approaching figure was an unfamiliar dark hulk in the shadowy woods, but the raised broadsword glinted a refracted moonlight off its blade in diamond-shaped shards of reflection. The medieval weapon made small loops in a nearly ritualistic preparation for the killing thrust. Its next devastating blow would destroy any living thing in its path.

Lyon tripped across an ankle-high root near his right foot. He plunged face forward into the ground. His forehead struck a rock and dozens of black dots swarmed across his vision. His body was drained. His vision clouded as he raised his arms in a futile attempt to ward off the impending sword thrust.

His adversary closed the distance between them. They

1

were now close enough that their feet were nearly touching.

An inappropriate thought surfaced. Historically, men led to the killing block tipped their executioner with gold to assure that the first blow was true and fatal.

The sword glinted in the moonlight as it slowly descended. He tensed in anticipation of the blow. The point sliced through the remains of his shirt.

The light was still too diffuse for him to make out the features of the dark figure looming above him. The only clear object was the broadsword, which sparkled in the dim light that seeped through the leaf cover.

'Why?' The word burst forth in an unfamiliar hoarse voice. He could hear the deep breathing of the figure above him, but there was no reply. He tensed again, waiting for the blow.

The apparition disappeared into the darkness as quickly as it had appeared. Lyon grasped a tree limb as he struggled to his feet. He swayed as he tried to focus his eyes. He was dizzy, and disoriented.

He took two steps and pitched forward into the darkness.

Police Chief Rocco Herbert slowed the police cruiser as he turned into the long drive that led to Nutmeg Hill. He unconsciously eased the handgun holstered at his hip an inch or two up and down to confirm that it was seated properly.

Bea Wentworth's early-morning long-distance phone call to his home had been worrisome. There was more than a hint of concern in her voice, an unusual condition for the usually unflappable state senator.

'They told me the phones were out of order, Rocco,' she had said. 'What bothers me is that I have a second line going into the house for my political calls, and for two phone lines to go out simultaneously doesn't make sense. If it weren't for the fact that Morgan is parked in our drive, I'd think the main line to the street was down. You know, Morgan's been getting those weird threats recently?'

'I've heard about them. He refused the guard the Middleburg Police offered to put at his house. You want me to check it out, Bea?' he had asked.

2

'I'd feel better. Would you mind terribly driving out to Nutmeg Hill on your way to work this morning to make sure everything is all right?'

His first thought had been to dispatch a patrol unit, but a glance at the bedside clock told him that he had time to make the trip himself. He could have coffee with his friend Lyon, and still get to the police station in time for his scheduled meeting with the town's first selectman. 'Sure. I'll be glad to. I'll leave as soon as I'm dressed. You want I should call you in Washington?' He picked up the tiny pen attached to the note pad on the night table next to the bed.

'You can't,' she had replied. 'I'm on the road right now, on my way back to Connecticut. I'd just feel better knowing you were checking things out.'

He pulled the cruiser to a stop immediately behind the RV parked near the home's front door. He eased from the car with his right hand resting lightly on the butt of his handgun.

The house was quiet. Bea had evidently driven her small sedan to Washington, and the only other vehicle besides the modified Winnebago in the drive was Lyon's ancient pickup truck, parked by the barn.

He walked slowly around the RV. Lyon Wentworth had told him how Warren Morgan, a professor at nearby Middleburg University, had changed the configurations of the vehicle until it hardly resembled the standard model. The front doors had been strengthened with interior braces and welded shut. All of the windows had been replaced with the special safety glass utilized on armored cars. Steel plates that could be lowered had been mounted over the living compartment windows. A steel shield had been welded under the chassis for added protection. The final result: a vehicle with all the protection of an army tank and the interior comforts of a hedonist's house trailer.

The only means of access into the vehicle was a single rear door which he pounded on with his fist. Near the door was a lock combination panel. 'Hey, Morgan! You in there? Anyone in there? Open up! Police!'

No answer.

3

He repeated the process several times before he shook his head and walked slowly toward the house.

Nutmeg Hill was located on a saucer-shaped promontory that rose a hundred feet above a sharp bend in the Connecticut River. The house was at the apex of this rise and was reached by a winding drive that twisted up from a secondary highway. High stands of pine marched along formal lanes on either side of the lawn. The structural lines of the house were dominated by a widow's walk that ran the length of the gambrel roof. Leaded glass windows reflected the early sun as it brimmed the hills to the east.

The Wentworths had purchased the property a number of years before. It had originally been constructed in the early nineteenth century by a successful sea captain. After the Civil War, the original family's fortunes faltered. The house began a slow process of decay until a last surviving spinster moved south and boarded the windows and doors. Vandals and weather hastened further deterioration. Lyon and Bea had discovered the building accidentally while on a walking trip. They had fallen in love with its secluded location and panoramic perch. They finally arranged a purchase through the estate of the deceased spinster. It had taken them years of painstaking labor to refurbish the house.

Rocco noticed that the front door was slightly ajar. As he slow approached it, a wind eddied up from the river and blew the door fully open.

'Hey, Lyon!' Rocco yelled. 'You in there?'

No answer.

He drew the revolver and braced his right wrist with his left hand as he stepped carefully through the doorway.

Police Chief Rocco Herbert was a large man with a craggy face. He was too big to be a professional football linebacker, although a guard or tackle's position might have been suitable. His six foot six frame carried closer to 300 than 200 pounds. His massive bulk did not slow his reflexes and he could move with a surprising alacrity if the situation warranted.

He went methodically through each of the twelve rooms. They were all unoccupied. The master bedroom was undisturbed, the king-size bed still neatly made. In the adjoining bathroom, he ran his fingers lightly over the surface of the stall shower wall and sink bowl. They were both dry and obviously had not been used since the day before.

His search was complete except for the widow's walk on the roof. He stood by the narrow door that led to the steps up the walk. In all his years of visits to Nutmeg Hill, he had never been on the widow's walk. He shrugged. What the hell, there's always a first time, he thought as he proceeded up the stairs with the service revolver tightly clutched in his hand.

The roof was deserted except for a solitary crow that immediately took flight at his approach. He stood by one of the chimneys and looked out over the side lawns, then toward the tree lines on either side of the house, and finally down toward the river. He saw a small motorboat proceeding downstream and a coastal tanker making its way upstream toward the tank farms near Hartford. In the opposite direction he could see a church spire on the Murphysville town green. The single-story police services building two blocks from the green was obscured by intervening trees, but he knew its exact location by instinct, just as he knew all the dimensions of his domain.

Movement by the edge of the pines to the north attracted his attention.

Lyon Wentworth, hunched and bloody, stumbled toward the house. In one hand he clutched the hilt of a long sword that he dragged across the grass.

'Lyon!' Rocco bellowed.

Lyon looked toward the house in a bewildered manner and continued his stumbling forward movement.

Rocco took the stairs two at a time and reached the front door as Lyon lurched through the entryway.

The broadsword clattered to the floor and Lyon leaned against the wall. His breath came in short gasps. It took a few minutes before he registered Rocco's presence. A half smile of recognition and relief crossed his face. 'My God, Rocco,' he said in a choked voice. 'Something happened to me out there last night and I'm not sure what.' He stumbled forward and grasped the stair banister with both hands.

5

Rocco noticed that the touch left bloody prints on the burnished wood. His friend's torn shirt was covered in blood, with streaks down the length of his khaki pants and across his face.

Rocco overcame his initial surprise and moved quickly to help his friend. He placed his hands on Lyon's shoulders and gently forced him down until he sat on the steps. 'Easy now. Do you know where you're hurt?'

'No.'

'I'm concerned about shock.' He strode down the hall into the living room, where he grasped the edge of a heavy window drape and yanked it from its runners. Bundling the material, he reached through the swinging door into the kitchen and snicked the phone from its wall mount.

'Damn,' he said into the dead phone as he recalled that the lines were out. Rocco hurried back to Lyon and began to wrap him in the drape. 'I'll get the first-aid kit from the car and radio for an ambulance. Hold on, old buddy, and we'll pull you through.'

'I don't think I'm hurt, Rocco. This isn't my blood.'

'You look like a fugitive from a fire fight. Are you sure you're all right? What in the hell happened?'

'I'm OK, just dazed,' Lyon insisted as he unwound himself from the drape and stumbled up the stairs toward the master bedroom.

Rocco followed as his friend stripped off his bloody clothes and dropped them in the center of the bedroom floor. Lyon stepped into the shower and turned the water on full force.

Police Chief Rocco Herbert stared down at the pile of bloody clothing heaped on the floor. He grimaced as he pulled out a mechanical pencil from his breast pocket. He inserted the point under the edge of the torn clothing and gingerly lifted the sport shirt and khaki pants into the acetate evidence bag he always carried folded in a rear pocket.

'You know, I could send this stuff to the state forensic lab for testing.' There was no answer from the man in the shower. 'Do you have any cuts? Perhaps a nosebleed that would account for the blood?' Still no answer. He sealed the evidence bag and continued staring at it. 'Can you hear me in there, Lyon? This could be damn important.'

The water was abruptly shut off. Lyon came out of the bathroom wearing a terry-cloth robe and toweling his hair. The shower seemed to have refreshed him to the point where his manner had begun a return to normalcy.

'There's not a cut on me except for a bruise on my forehead,' Lyon said. 'That isn't my blood on the clothes.' He threw the towel toward a hamper in the corner of the bathroom. It missed and draped over the sink, where it hung loosely toward the floor.

'Then whose blood is it?'

Lyon Wentworth lowered himself on to a straight chair near the mirrored clothes closet, where he dressed in khaki pants and a sports shirt similar to the bloody clothes in the bag at Rocco's feet. The two men in the bedroom of the house on the promontory high above the Connecticut River were a study in contrast. Lyon was a tall slender man with a shock of sandy brown hair that often fell in an unruly forelock. A children's book writer, he was well known for the Wobblies, a pair of benign monsters who specialized in adventure and rescue. His fey grin, usually accompanied by a somewhat bemused look, often made him appear distracted.

'Are you going to tell me what's going on?' Rocco snapped.

'I think I've pieced together what happened to me last night,' Lyon said.

'Where did you get that gigantic pig sticker you dragged across the lawn?' Rocco pressed.

Lyon shook his head in a gesture of confusion. 'It was evidently left by my attacker. The whole bit had the feel of a nightmare, but it was real enough.'

'Please explain.'

'Since I dragged the sword home, I obviously wasn't dreaming. I think I may have been drugged with some sort of hallucinogen.'

'Tell me what you remember.'

As he finished dressing, Lyon described the attack in the dark by the hooded figure with the sword. 'I thought I was going to be killed,' he concluded.

7

'And you have no idea who it was?'

'Its face was obscured by the cowl of the robe.'

'Could it have been Morgan playing another one of his sadistic games?'

'Not tall enough for Morgan,' Lyon responded.

It was Rocco's turn to shake his head. 'People running around in the middle of the night waving crusader swords? What is this?'

'When I woke up, the sword was sticking upright in the ground not ten feet from where I was,' Lyon said. 'It was late and dark. Whoever attacked me thought I was Morgan. They pursued me until they discovered at the last moment that I was not Morgan. That's when they backed off and left the sword and blood as a sign of some sort. If we have the blood tested, I wager it's not human blood.'

'Maybe. What about Morgan? Isn't that his RV in the drive?'

'He sleeps and eats in there,' Lyon answered. 'But the way he's got that thing constructed, he's safe enough.'

'Is he in there now?'

'As far as I know.'

'He didn't open the door for me. When I first arrived, I pounded on the door loud enough to wake the . . . I think we had better have a look.'

Lyon led the way down the wide stairs to the front door that led into the drive. 'How about coffee before we wake Morgan up?'

'Come on! I can't do anything until I see if that guy is all right.'

'I guarantee it,' Lyon said. 'He gave me the guided tour the other day and I'd feel safe in that RV during a war.'

Rocco circled the Winnebago. 'Well, I hope so, because I can't get inside it. I think we had better find out if we have a crime scene here. I checked all the rooms and didn't find a thing. Was anyone else here overnight?'

'No. There were a few people over for drinks and barbecue but everyone left except Morgan. He locked himself in his RV fairly early on. Bea's away at a conference for women legislators in Washington and will be back sometime later today.'

'I know. She's concerned about the threats to Morgan and called me at home this morning. She said she'd been trying to get in touch with you for hours, but the phones are out of order.' Rocco pounded on the side of the RV. 'Morgan! I kid you not, open the door.'

Rocco appraised the modified RV again. 'I estimate that doing what he did to this vehicle would have set me back about two years' salary.'

'I know the amount of your salary, since it's in the town's annual report, so make that about three years' worth.'

Rocco began to impatiently pound on the side of the Winnebago. 'Damn it, Morgan! Open this can of tuna fish or you're getting a citation. You hear me? It's going to cost you a fine.'

'Morgan is contrary. He opens up when and if he chooses to,' Lyon said.

'Oh, yeah,' Rocco said with a twinge of anger. 'Well, I think something's happened out here. Look at that.' He pointed to a thin trail of blood across the drive that the sword had left as Lyon dragged it to the house. 'Something's damn sure coming down unless you were hunting rodents with that crusader impaler.'

Lyon shook his head. 'You're an alarmist. I'm still convinced that's animal blood meant for a warning. Morgan's OK unless someone put a lot of pounds of plastic explosives underneath the RV, which they obviously haven't. He modified the thing for protection and I think he succeeded.'

Rocco stalked around the vehicle as he examined it for damage or means of entry. 'Hell, I don't know. Maybe they gassed him through the air vents or something.'

'He anticipated that possibility and installed an air-filtration system. It's built into that air-conditioning unit on the roof.'

'Isn't there a way to get into this damn thing?'

'It's a combination lock and only Morgan and I have the combination,' Lyon said.

Rocco stopped to glare at his friend. 'This is all a set-up to get me, right? Crusader swords and impregnable vehicles are Morgan's idea of funning me, right? Listen, you two wise-guys, I have a meeting with the first selectman in half an hour and she is trying to cut my budget. No more fun and games this morning or I will get really grumpy.'

'No games, Rocco,' Lyon said.

'If you have the combination, open the damn thing. Under the circumstances, I can hardly leave the premises until I am satisfied that Morgan is alive and well.'

Lyon punched two numbers into the combination panel next to the door, cleared them and inserted another set of three. He cleared those and hesitated. 'I forgot it.'

Rocco pointed to the long sword on the floor just inside the vestibule. 'You see that thing. Forget your hooded apparitions; I am going to cut your head off with it. You forgot it! Wake up, Lyon!'

'Come to think of it, I do believe I made a note of the numbers in my study.'

Lyon hurried through the house and into his study down the hall from the kitchen. Sitting at his desk in front of the computer console, he pulled out the secretary drawer. Years ago he had taped a piece of yellow typewriter paper on the pull-out and had made a practice of jotting down serial numbers there that he never seemed able to remember. These included their car and truck marker plate numbers, his social security number, their safe deposit box number, and the other useful numerology of their life. Scrawled in the far right-hand corner was an unlabeled series he had recently written. He remembered the sequence as the RV's door combination. He glanced at it and hurried back to the drive.

'Got it,' he said to Rocco as he punched the numbers into a combination panel to the right of the door. 'Have it open in a sec.'

The door swung open and Rocco stepped inside and stopped. His body blocked the entrance. 'Good God!' he said in a low voice.

'What is it?' Lyon asked, suddenly aware of the alarm in his friend's voice.

Rocco stepped back out of the Winnebago and leaned against the side of the vehicle with both hands pressed against the metal. Lyon started inside until Rocco's hand grasped

10

his shoulder. 'Don't,' the large chief said. 'You don't have to. I do.'

Lyon shook off the restraint and stepped into the RV. Once inside, he saw what Rocco meant. The chief re-entered and stood by his side.

'He's been butchered,' Lyon said.

'And that sword you dragged across the lawn is what probably did it,' Rocco said.

'This is impossible,' Lyon said in an attempt to deny the undeniable. 'There was no way for anyone to get inside to do this.'

Two

Lyon Wentworth sat on a wrought-iron chair on the patio by the parapet at Nutmeg Hill. He looked, without seeing, at the hills bracketing the Connecticut River as it wound its way toward Long Island Sound.

'This is impossible, you know,' he repeated to Rocco, who sat nearby on the parapet wall. 'There was no way anyone could get inside that van to murder Morgan.'

Rocco looked past his distraught friend, toward the rapidly filling driveway. The accumulation of cars and vans was in response to his radio call to the town dispatcher. Near the drive entrance a second Murphysville cruiser was parked on the grass while its driver directed traffic at the secondary highway below the house. An ambulance passed several state police cruisers, a state forensics lab truck, and the medical examiner's car before stopping near the RV. Two uniformed attendants exited the ambulance and casually opened the rear doors to pull out a folded gurney. They weren't in any hurry, since they knew it was a homicide.

'You're the ones who always say there's an explanation for everything,' Rocco said as another state police cruiser occupied by two corporals and a captain turned up the drive with an impatient honk. 'Oh, Christ,' Rocco mumbled. 'Here comes my brother-in-law the Lone Ranger with his two Tontos.'

Lyon stood so abruptly that his chair fell backward on the fieldstone with a clatter. 'There's got to be a way someone got into that RV and I'm going to find it.' He started off the patio toward the driveway.

Rocco took two quick strides. His hand curled over Lyon's shoulder. 'Let the pros handle it.'

Lyon abruptly halted and turned toward Rocco. 'Is that a suggestion or a command?'

'A little bit of both. You can't go in there now. It's a crime scene.'

'Am I allowed back in my own house?'

'There's a uniform in the doorway who will keep all un-authorized persons from the premises until it's released.'

'You're beginning to sound like an official manual,' Lyon said.

'These guys seem to have a pretty good handle on things,' Rocco replied. 'They'll wrap it up as quickly as possible and depart.'

'What I'm beginning to wonder,' Lyon said, 'is whether I'm going to be required to go with them when they leave.'

'That depends,' Rocco replied

Both men watched the medical examiner leave the RV and give the signal to the two ambulance attendants to remove the body. A forensics tech came out the front door, carefully carrying the sword cradled in his arms. He had fashioned a large evidence bag from several smaller ones until the weapon was completely encased in transparent acetate.

Captain Norbert of the state police followed the medical examiner out of the RV. Both men examined the encased sword in the tech's arms until the doctor gave an affirmative nod.

'Looks like the sword was it,' Rocco said softly.

'If that blood on my clothing matches Morgan's . . .' Lyon left the remainder of the thought unspoken.

Norbert, deep in thought, walked slowly toward the patio steps. He was followed by a corporal. He nodded at Rocco. 'Chief Herbert.'

'Captain Courageous, I presume,' Rocco replied.

'Cut the crap,' the captain snapped.

Norbert was a bantam-size man. He had barely qualified for the trooper height requirements, but, as the years passed, he compensated for this lack by increasing the girth of his upper body. He now appeared to be slightly top-heavy. His forward momentum had matured into a minor strut that seemed necessary to propel his pyknic physique forward.

'Here they are, Captain.' The second corporal hurried to the captain's side and handed him the acetate bag containing Lyon's bloody clothing. Norbert took it with a grimace and thrust it toward Lyon.

'This your clothing, Wentworth?'

'Yes.'

Norbert handed the evidence back to the corporal. 'They tell me you were wandering around the woods carrying that sword.'

'Yes.'

'The medical examiner informs me that it might be the murder weapon. Lab tests will or will not confirm that.' The last remarks were directed directly at Rocco. 'His prints are probably smeared all over the damn thing.'

Lyon seemed oblivious to the remarks. 'Since the death threats against Morgan began—'

'That's Warren Morgan, the victim,' Rocco said.

Norbert snapped his fingers and the first corporal began to take rapid notes.

'Morgan,' Lyon continued, 'has recently been living in his recreational vehicle. It's a radically modified Winnebago. It's those structural changes that complicate matters.'

'What does that mean?'

'I was never quite sure what kind of attack he expected,' Lyon said. 'He had modified it until the whole thing became a rolling fortress.'

'There was absolutely no way to get into that vehicle when Morgan had it buttoned up,' Rocco said. 'And on the night of his death it was shut up tighter than a Sherman tank. Theoretically there was no way anyone could get in without his permission. And since he always locked the door when he left, if Morgan came outside voluntarily and was killed in the open, there would be no way to get his body back inside.'

'But you somehow managed to open it and find the body?' Norbert said skeptically.

'Morgan had installed a combination lock on the Winnebago's side door,' Rocco said. 'He changed the number settings yesterday and, as far as we know, Lyon was the only person who had the combination to that lock. He's the one who opened it for me.'

'How cooperative of him,' Norbert said. 'Getting this down?' he snapped at the corporal.

'Yes, sir. Every word.'

'Let's proceed with the matter of the death threats. Exactly who was threatening Morgan?'

Lyon looked out over the hills. 'It's a rather extensive list. I suppose you might start with two literature professors from Middleburg University, and include his half-brother and sister.'

'Then there's the Satan crew,' Rocco said. 'They call themselves the Brotherhood of Beelzebub. We understand from the broadsides they posted that a few dozen of them have sworn a sacred vow to kill Morgan.'

'Satan worshipers?' Norbert asked. 'Do we know who or where they are?'

'We haven't been able to track them down yet,' Rocco said. 'Probably a bunch of disgruntled college dropouts. The broadsword fits rather nicely into their ritualistic beliefs. The chief mucky muck of the Brotherhood of Beelzebub, whatever they call him, recently placed a hundred-grand bounty on Morgan.'

'The brother and sister were after the control of the trust fund,' Lyon added. 'But I don't know how much money is involved there.'

'Tell me about these Beelzebub characters. Why were they so upset?' Norbert asked.

'Their leader was displeased, and that's putting it mildly, with a series of articles that Morgan wrote for *New Forward* magazine. That really set them off,' Lyon said.

'Some sort of pungent postmodern criticism, I suppose.'

'It began with a literary pastiche called "Bloody Rights or Bloody Rites". It satirized them as being all puerile bluster and no action.'

'They were not amused,' Rocco added.

'What are the faculty members after?' Norbert asked.

'Morgan was chairman of a department, and there's a battle over the appointment to a new endowed chair,' Lyon

15

said. 'The faculty takes that sort of business rather seriously.'

'Captain,' the second corporal said. 'There's a civilian van coming up the drive.'

Norbert snapped around to see a television remote unit with a satellite dish on the roof approaching. It was stopped fifty yards from the house by a Murphysville police officer. 'Oh, Christ!' the state police captain said. 'How do these paparazzi do it? If we were that efficient, the crime rate would drop thirty per cent.' He went through the open French doors that led into the living room. When no one followed, he gave an impatient signal to Rocco. 'Come on, let's get a rough statement down before we get buried by the reporters. Keep the media away from the house!' he yelled to one of his corporals. He put his arm around Lyon's shoulder. 'I hope there is a logical explanation for everything that's happened here, Mr Wentworth. By the way, where is Senator Beatrice Wentworth?'

'She's out of town,' Lyon said.

'Let's get your feedback on what we've got so far,' Norbert said. He read from his corporal's notes and made slashing checks at each item. 'The deceased was Warren Morgan, chairman of the English department at Middleburg University. He was evidently a man of exceptionally poor social skills. The deceased was under some sort of ritualistic sentence of death by some cult of the devil. Two days ago he parked his modified Winnebago in the Wentworths' drive. Last night, prior to the murder, there was a small gathering for drinks and barbecue at the Wentworth home. Present were two teachers from the university, Morgan's half-brother and sister, along with the sister's boyfriend. The victim, Morgan, and the host, Wentworth, were also present.

'At some point during the night or early morning, Wentworth was possibly drugged. While in a confused state of mind he was pursued by a hooded individual waving a large sword.' Norbert looked up at Lyon and slowly shook his head before continuing. 'Wentworth evidently passed out during this attack. He awakened at about the time Chief Herbert arrived to check out a phone request from Mrs

Wentworth, who was not present during these activities.' He gave a baleful look at Lyon. 'You are evidently a very sound sleeper. Morgan was last seen alive when he retired to his armored vehicle parked in the Wentworths' drive. He was observed closing and locking the combination door that led into the vehicle. This morning Chief Herbert discovered Mr Wentworth dazed and wandering toward the house wearing blood-smeared clothing and carrying a large antique sword. The medical examiner states that the deceased's injuries could have been made by that type of sword. Forensic tests on the blood spatters are yet to be performed. The deceased's body was found inside the armored vehicle. Access into said vehicle was gained by the only other person besides the victim who possessed the combination to the door, Lyon Wentworth.'

Lyon nodded. 'That seems correct. I know this all sounds rather bizarre,' Lyon said tiredly.

Norbert glared at Rocco and gestured toward the hallway. Both men stepped into the kitchen. As soon as the senior police officers left the room, the attitude of the remaining corporals moved from attentive note-taking to guardianship. They shifted positions and seemed alert to any abrupt movements by Lyon.

'You know, Herbert, I don't really need this,' Norbert said. 'This guy's wife is one of the most prominent state legislators in Connecticut. She's a friend of the governor, at least one of our US senators, and my commissioner. On top of that, this guy comes up with a story that makes me want to believe in the tooth fairy. Jesus, I can't win on this one.'

'He happens to be my closest friend, Norbie,' Rocco said.

'The guy, Wentworth, he's not in local politics or connected to the financial community, is he?'

'No. He's still writing children's books, mostly about things he calls his Wobbly monsters,' Rocco said.

'I hope he's not a goddamn intellectual.'

'He's a trustee of Middleburg University.'

'Jesus, why did you involve me? A hell of a brother-in-law you are. In the past you've always been the one to fight for your jurisdictional rights to keep us out of a case.'

'I couldn't take jurisdiction this time, Norbie. I'll do

anything in the world I can to help Lyon, but my conflict of interest is so obvious the media would hang us both if I stay on the case. That would do more harm than good for Lyon.' Norbert sighed. 'God. I'm stuck with a no-win deal here.' He shook himself as if to ward off further onslaughts. 'We're knee-deep in barn droppings, Rocco. You neatly disqualified yourself, but how long do you think it's going to take for the media to find out that you and I are related by marriage? About ten seconds, that's how long. So, I'm warning you. I want any information you have, or your conduct goes straight to a one-man grand jury. What else do you have? And I mean really what else!'

Rocco's craggy facial lines seemed to harden into rocky faults as his inner torment became obvious to the state police officer. 'There's been talk recently.'

'Of what? Damn it all, man, spit it out!'

'Forget it.' Rocco started back toward the living room.

'Forget hell!' Norbert grabbed the chief's arm and whirled him around. Although he had to tilt his head to look up at Rocco, it didn't seem to diminish his belligerency. 'It'll come out eventually. You know it always does. What do you know?'

'It's unconfirmed. So forget it.'

'Something about Senator Wentworth playing house with the deceased?' Norbert asked.

'Where'd you get that crap?'

'From your wife, my sister. And it could be true.'

'It's just stupid talk that Martha picked up somewhere, and I can't possibly believe it.'

'It's a possible motive.'

'Hell, Norbie, it's only beauty-parlor gossip.'

'We don't have to prove motive, Rocco,' Norbert said. 'All we have to produce is probable cause as to who done it. The motive bit narrows down our suspect list, which in this case seems to have a single name on it.'

'There are others who had it in for Morgan,' Rocco said.

'Your friend in the living room was in possession of what will probably turn out to be the murder weapon. He was covered in blood. You tell me that when you found him he seemed dazed and confused. He had the opportunity, since

18

he possessed the door combination, and he had a possible motive. Jesus, Rocco, the only thing left to get is his confession.'

'Assuming the forensics check out.'

'I would be amazed if they didn't,' Norbert said as he started through the swinging door.

'At this point Lyon had best shut up,' Rocco said.

Again Norbert performed his belligerent pivot to approach Rocco. 'You keep your mouth shut? In fact, why don't you get the hell out of here, since this is my case?'

'There's a matter of reading his rights,' Rocco said.

'When I make the arrest. A couple more loose ends and then we make the arrest and go for the confession. That's when he gets his Miranda. But I'm warning you, Herbert. Back off and don't interfere.' His anger seemed to increase the angle of his strut as he stormed back to the living room with Rocco reluctantly following. 'A few more loose ends, Mr Wentworth,' Captain Norbert said in an even and reasonable voice. 'I assume that the deceased was more than a casual acquaintance of yours.'

'At one time I taught in his department. We've known each other for nearly fifteen years.'

'And how long have you known of the deceased's affair with Senator Wentworth?'

Lyon's face rapidly merged through a series of emotions. The sequence began with blank incomprehension which shifted temporarily into anger and finally humor. 'You've got to be kidding?'

'I do not joke,' the captain replied.

'That's for sure,' Rocco agreed.

Lyon laughed. 'My wife is a very independent person, but Morgan . . .' He laughed again.

'Let's go back to when you were on the Middleburg faculty,' Norbert said.

'We were both instructors in the same department before I resigned to pursue my career as a freelance writer.'

'I wanted to get to that,' the captain said. 'You write anything we might know?'

'My most successful book was one I did a few years ago

during the Bicentennial. You may have heard of *Nancy Goes to Mount Vernon.*'

Norbert made no effort to conceal his disdain. 'Years ago we used to confiscate filth like that. I remember one hot number in particular called *Debbie Does Dallas.*'

Rocco was unable to control himself any longer. 'For God's sake! The man writes children's literature.'

Norbert shrugged. 'Whatever. We can assume that Senator Wentworth knew the deceased for an equal amount of time, that is to say fifteen years?'

'You know, Captain, at this point, you've really lost me,' Lyon said.

Norbert nodded. 'I see. Can we assume that you are terminating this interview, Mr Wentworth?'

'You may so assume,' Lyon answered.

'In that case,' Norbert said as he stood before Lyon, 'I must warn you.' He held out his hand toward one of the ever present corporals, who promptly slapped a laminated Rights Warning card in his palm.

Rocco pushed Captain Norbert aside and clicked a hand-cuff over Lyon's right wrist. 'It's my collar, Norbie. You are under arrest,' he said to Lyon. 'You have the right to remain silent. You are not required to say anything to us at any time or to . . .'

'That's ridiculous,' Bea Wentworth said from the French doors. 'He didn't kill Morgan. I did!'

20

Three

'What in the hell is going on here?' Captain Norbert's face flushed a deep red. His quick angry glance included everyone in the room. 'Are you deliberately creating a circus here, Herbert? What sort of stupid games are you people playing?'

'I'm making it my collar, Norbie,' Rocco answered. 'Wentworth is my prisoner.'

'Come with me, Chief,' Norbert said as he gestured Rocco back into the kitchen. As soon as they were alone, the state police captain exploded in a paroxysm of whispered rage. 'What are you doing? Are you trying to taint all our actions out here today? This is unprofessional behavior of the worst magnitude and the state's attorney will be so informed.'

'You wear blinkers, Norbie,' Rocco responded. 'And you always have. Once you zero in on a suspect, you move the rocks of hell to gather more evidence for your conviction, but never look around the corner for another suspect. Your blinkers don't allow you to see beyond the one you've decided on, Captain. You've always been that way and so are a lot of other cops.'

'Your fear of conflict of interest seems to have flown with the rest of your senses.'

'My best friend is going to twist in the wind if I don't help him. I know in the depths of my being that he is innocent.'

'Innocent! I've got everything except a confession or eyewitness. And tell me what in hell the senator is pulling?'

'Pulling?'

'She's evidently playing games, unless . . . .' He stopped in mid-sentence, to continue in a conspiratorial tone. 'Unless they are both in it together. The family Wentworth knocked Morgan off and will now cover for each other. I've ridden that merry-go-round before.'

'I'm buying Lyon some time, Norbie. Now go along with me on this and don't hound the state's attorney for your warrant.'

'I'll be in his office a half hour after I leave here. If you don't have that man arraigned no later than tomorrow, you are in deep shit, Herbert.'

Rocco turned without a word and returned to the living room. Norbert followed, but his voice dropped two unctuous registers as he approached Bea. 'There are circumstances here, Senator, that—'

'I demand to be remanded into custody,' Bea said. 'I insist on being fingerprinted and shoved in a lineup.'

'We don't have lineups in Murphysville,' Rocco said tiredly. 'Everyone knows everyone else.'

'Isn't anyone interested in my confession?' Bea asked. 'Take those cuffs off Lyon and slap them on me.'

'Oh, Christ, the media is going to crucify all of us,' Norbert mumbled.

'You haven't had any firearms training, Bea,' Rocco said. 'Only a trained marksman could have pulled off the shot that killed Morgan.'

'Nice try, Rocco,' she replied. 'Except that I know he was killed with a sword. It so happens that I was on the fencing team in college. You can verify that from my yearbook.'

'Morgan's fatal wounds were hardly the result of fancy épée thrusts.'

'The saber was always my weapon of choice,' Bea responded.

Norbert was fascinated by this pert, feisty woman who stood defiantly before them. Bea Wentworth was slightly under medium height, with a figure that might be described as petite except for the fullness of her breasts and hips. Her short hair was worn in a fashion that bracketed her face and gave her a gamin-like appearance. This innocent quality was usually belied by the darting intelligence and intensity of her eyes. Norbert had known her casually for years, and had

22

followed her political career from state representative to secretary of the state and then state senator. He had also watched several television interviews when she was spokesperson for a cause or sponsor of specific legislation.

Patrolman Jamie Martin of the Murphysville police force stuck his head through the French doors. 'Call for you on the radio, Chief. Dispatcher can't get through on land lines. He says the first selectman is really pissed that you missed her meeting.' Rocco groaned and followed the officer out.

'I was told you were in Washington, Senator Wentworth,' Norbert muttered in a polite voice far below his usual interview standards.

'I left last night and drove straight home to Connecticut.'

'Do I handcuff one of them or both?' the taller of the state police corporals asked.

'Hold on and let me sort this out,' Norbert answered. He struggled to regain his interview dominance. As a consequence, his next question was asked in a manner more harsh than intended. 'And you were somehow able to open a locked RV door? Once inside, you managed to overpower Morgan?'

'I knew where the door's combination was kept. It doesn't take much strength to murder a sleeping man.'

'You had the combination? How strange!' Norbert said as he searched back through his notes. 'And how did you manage to obtain the combination? I understood that the lock was recently changed and only Lyon and Morgan knew the new setting.'

'It was quite simple actually. I merely went to where Lyon kept the combination and let myself in,' Bea said.

Norbert looked at Lyon. 'Where Lyon kept the combination? Where he'd written it down for the world to see?'

'Not hardly everyone,' Bea said. 'I'm the only one who knows that Lyon can't remember things like his own social security number. He records all his important numbers in the same place: on the pull-out shelf at his desk. All manner of our life's numerology are scribbled on a yellow piece of typewriter paper he scotch-taped there years ago.'

Lyon blanched in a manner so noticeable that Norbert and his corporals exchanged glances.

23

'Is what she says true?' the state police captain asked Lyon.

'Well, yes. Bea knows I jot down all sorts of numbers in that particular place.'

'Including the RV door combination?'

'Yes.' He turned to his wife. 'Nice try, honey, but I really don't need you to do this for me.'

'Let's get back to work. I believe we were discussing your affair with the deceased, Senator Wentworth.'

'My what?'

'We were about to develop detailed facts concerning your liaison with Morgan. The affair is a rather important element in this case, since it provides motive. A motive which someone brought to the attention of the state police. It is almost immaterial which one of you was the actual perpetrator, since the existence of the affair provides a possible motive for either or both of you.'

Bea looked startled. 'I don't mean to appear hopelessly naive, but what affair are you referring to?'

'Were you involved with the deceased?'

'Captain, Morgan was a very talented man, in some ways a very interesting man. Believe me when I say that a sexual relationship with him would be as likely as my seduction by Rasputin.'

'Will you please answer the question directly? Were you lovers?'

'That's even more preposterous than her killing him,' Lyon said.

'We have known him for years,' Bea said. 'We met him during the early days of our marriage, when Lyon and Morgan were new instructors at the university.'

'Then you were good friends with the man?'

'I won't say friends,' Bea replied. 'I'm not sure anyone was really friends with Morgan. Perhaps longtime acquaintances would be a better term.'

Captain Norbert sighed. 'To move on. Can you tell me where you were yesterday and last night, Senator?'

'I was at a convention of women legislators in Washington DC,' Bea said. 'I was at meetings all day yesterday and attended the banquet last night. I drove home immediately after the dinner.'

'Nope.' Rocco stood in the doorway shaking his head. 'Nice try, but no way, Beatrice. You spent the night with a United States senator.'

'What senator?' Norbert asked softly. 'Is he, pray tell, from the State of Massachusetts?'

Lyon shook his head in disgust at the man's prurient interest. 'She was probably with Senator Katherine Turman, who has a husband and five kids.'

Bea shrugged.

Norbert looked at Rocco. 'Was it Turman?'

'Yep. I patched through to our station phone and it took a single call to establish that she spent the night at the home of our state's junior senator. She also phoned Nutmeg Hill repeatedly last night and again early this morning. The house phone was reported out of order each time. She told Senator Turman that she was very concerned because of the recent death threats against Morgan. This morning she phoned me at home. If we need her, Senator Turman will make a great witness, but the phone company records will establish that the early call to my house came from a pay phone on Interstate Ninety-Five.'

'Her deposition will do,' Norbert said. 'I'm glad you cleared that little matter up, Rocco. Now, will you take your cuffs off your friend so we can formally charge him?'

'You don't seem to understand, Norbie. Mr Wentworth is my prisoner. He will be formally booked in Murphysville and arraigned in superior court in a few days.'

'You're out to lunch.' Norbert turned to his two corporals, who seemed poised for instructions. 'Take our prisoner to the car.'

Both troopers immediately moved toward Lyon until Rocco inserted himself in their way. 'You guys are going to have to come through me.'

The taller of the state police officers, who was still six inches shorter than Rocco, turned toward his commanding officer. 'Captain?'

'You have just shot your career down the tube, big man,'

25

Norbert said. 'My sister will probably end up on welfare.' He stalked out the doors and down from the patio towards the cruiser parked in the drive.

'I think you've created a mess for yourself,' Lyon said to Rocco.

Bea stood outside the French doors, looking down the drive. 'Norbie is talking to the television crew. There's one guy with a microphone and another with a camera. I think they're interviewing him.'

Rocco closed his eyes momentarily and then looked up at Lyon. 'I would imagine that I am in deep, but you, old buddy, are so far down in a hole that you can't even see the top. Once you get in the clutches of a police bureaucracy that's convinced you're guilty, you won't even get bail. They'll stop looking for anything except evidence that will hang you even higher.'

'It looks that bad?' Lyon asked.

'Don't be naive. Those guys have you convicted. I've bought a little time. If I don't take you into superior court for arraignment in a few days, the state's attorney will send Norbie a warrant, and there's no way I can fight that. We had best make good use of the little time we have.'

'To find out who killed Morgan,' Lyon said.

'I'm sure there's not another person in this world who knows that Lyon keeps the numerology of his life on that paper in the desk,' Bea said. 'So there must be another way into that RV. Why don't we start by finding out how Morgan was killed?'

'That makes sense,' Lyon said as they left the house through the patio. They saw the RV, its front wheels raised up by a tow truck, start down the drive.

'What are they doing?' Bea asked.

'They've impounded it and are taking it to the state garage for evidence examination,' Rocco said.

'Then we don't get to go through it,' Lyon said.

'Not at this point,' Rocco replied. 'Let me get the TV guys off the property.' He moved quickly down the drive toward the television station's van.

Lyon walked along the edge of the house and glanced up

26

at the gutters. He reversed direction and moved a dozen feet away from the corner of the house nearest the drive and stooped to pick up the severed ends of telephone lines. 'I knew it had to be cut outside the house,' he told her. They walked back to the corner of the building where the phone lines had entered the dwelling. He stood on the seat of a wrought-iron bench near the wall and found that he could reach up to the port where the line went into the building. 'Easy enough, huh? Anyone could have cut it. All of us were either in the kitchen, study, or the far side on the rear patio by the parapet. It would have taken only seconds for someone to come around the house, hop on the bench and reach up to cut the lines.'

'It could have been done by someone not at the party,' Bea said. 'You wouldn't have noticed anyone coming up the drive or across the lawn.'

Lyon nodded. 'True.'

They were silent as they looked down the drive toward the entrance, where Rocco was arguing with the television crew. It was obvious that he had prevailed, as they were beginning to repack their equipment.

'Until last night our biggest problem was Camelot over there,' Bea said as she looked toward a high-rise building under construction on the corner of the promontory. Three floors of steel superstructure had already topped the tallest pine trees. A large crane squatting next to the building lifted steel girders to waiting iron workers who nonchalantly walked the narrow high beams.

They knew that the construction was a pricy, trendy condominium. Each unit would come equipped with a spectacular river view. The extra proposed amenities took up half a page in their brochure, and included bridle paths, tennis and paddle courts, a health club and indoor pool.

As the nearest and largest property owners in the area, the town knew they opposed the project. They beat it back twice. The developers knew they'd fight it to death at future public hearings.

The builder waited patiently for two years until the Wentworths took an extended trip to Europe and then rammed a variance through the Zoning Board.

Rocco stood at the bottom of the patio steps with an end of the cut telephone lines. 'Let's recreate your story,' he said. 'A person, who you cannot identify, threatened you with a sword.'

Lyon pointed to a stand of pine trees that began fifty yards from the side of the house. 'It happened over there.'

Bea Wentworth watched the two men walk across the lawn toward the tree line. Lyon had to look up to speak to the taller Rocco. A breeze unexpectedly swirled in off the river and ruffled Lyon's hair. She automatically brushed the edge of a hand across her own forehead in an exact duplication of the gesture her husband performed two dozen yards away. Her tight smile reflected a nostalgic wistfulness. She knew him so intimately that even his small unconscious gestures and the other nuances that create a unique person were familiar.

At the tree line, Lyon looked over his shoulder and saw his wife enter the house. It was apparent that she'd remained outside to watch them cross the field. He wondered what she'd been thinking.

'Are you with me, Lyon?' Rocco said.

Lyon refocused his thoughts. 'Yes, sorry. Last night, I was returning to the house after helping someone remove a car from a ditch when this thing came out of nowhere. It was dark, but in the moonlight I could see light refractions from the sword blade. I fell.'

'Let's back up from that point,' Rocco said. 'Start with the early evening and tell me exactly what happened. Include every detail you can recall, no matter how inconsequential it might seem.'

'Early last night, while it was still light, I was on the patio having drinks with Ernest Harnell,' Lyon said . . .

Four

'I'm Ernest Hemingway's bastard son, but you know that.'
Ernest Harnell put one foot up on Nutmeg Hill's low
parapet and struck what he considered a heroic pose. He
peered across the Connecticut River, which far below them
meandered toward Long Island Sound.

Lyon tilted a wrought-iron patio chair back on its legs as
he braced his feet against the wall and socially lied. 'No.
Actually, I don't believe you've ever mentioned it before.'
His companion's jaw imperceptibly tightened without
breaking his distant gaze. Lyon wondered if Ernest was
checking Spanish Loyalist troop positions across the river,
or watching long columns of the retreating Italian army at
Caporetto. He couldn't resist an impish impulse. 'I see a lot
of those Hemingway trucks on the Interstates. I would
suppose that there would be a rather large estate involved if
you were legitimized.'

Ernest immediately broke off his posturing as he snapped
his head around to glare down at Lyon. 'I hardly meant that
branch of the family. I speak of the writer. The Nobel Prize
laureate.'

'In that case, I do see a marked family resemblance,' Lyon
agreed. He failed to add that it was more than a genetic
familiarity of features. Ernest Harnell wore a short white
beard and sprouted a round paunch cultivated to the exact
dimensions familiar in the author's later photographs. His
round face mimicked a typical Hemingway set, which was
usually accentuated by a baseball cap, although tonight's
head covering was the only slightly less usual safari hat. It
was a studied imitation that created a close look-alike of the
older writer.

Harnell's face brightened. 'You do see it then?'

'It's unmistakable. There's a remarkably close similarity.' Lyon looked up at a formation of scudding off-white clouds crossing directly overhead. He was rather surprised to see his two imaginary Wobblies fly in perfect formation to a position just below the cloud layer. To his further astonishment, the two benign monsters began flying extremely complex patterns of outside loops. They had both positioned their front paws at right angles to their bodies in an imitation of wings. Their hind feet were pressed closely together, with the claws acting as ailerons and their long tails as rudders. Their aerial acrobatics were perfectly executed. He reflected on these surprising maneuvers, since during all the years he had written about his monster creations, he had never before realized that they could actually fly. Perhaps this was only a temporary aberration.

'It doesn't mean a damn thing to him,' Ernest said with an unmistakable tone of deep belligerence.

'Well, that's understandable,' Lyon answered. 'Hemingway's been dead for a number of years now.'

'I don't mean the writer. I mean Morgan.' He gestured toward the driveway, where a long RV was parked. 'When's he coming out of his goddamn Trojan horse? Or could we be so lucky that he's been entombed in there forever?'

'I haven't seen him all day,' Lyon said. 'He told me yesterday that he had a journal deadline, so he's probably sealed himself inside to get some work done. Another drink, Ernest?'

'Never ease off till the soldier's dead.' He reached for his empty glass balanced on the edge of the parapet and handed it to Lyon. 'For Christ's sake, build a man's drink this time, Went. Fix one like they mix them at Sloppy Joe's Bar in Key West.'

Lyon stepped through the French doors into the living room and over to where the bar cart was parked. He smiled as he carefully mixed a potent double for his guest. He held the drink up to examine it in the light and decided it was not of a hue acceptable at Sloppy Joe's. He laced it with more liquor until it darkened to an acceptable shade.

'As a matter of curiosity, Ernest, where did your mother meet Hemingway?' he called through the doors.

'I was conceived during a romantic afternoon in Hong Kong. Papa was in China to cover the Chinese-Japanese War. My mother was the daughter of missionaries and was attending a convent school in Hong Kong. On that particular afternoon she was having tea at an outdoor café . . . She was very young, and in those days Papa was really quite handsome. He graciously commented on her beauty and she coyly responded. One thing led to another that exquisite day and . . .'

Lyon returned to the patio and gave Ernest his fresh drink. 'All this happened in one afternoon?'

'That's all it takes, Wentworth.'

'So I've heard.'

'They were only able to share a few precious hours together. Their love affair may have been brief, but the height of their passion made up for its brevity.'

'I'm amazed that your mother would discuss these intimate details with her child.'

'Mother was too much the lady of the old school to talk about her sexuality. She never revealed any intimate details, but there were enough facts for me to piece together what actually happened.'

'Ernest, did your mother ever specifically say that she had an affair with Hemingway and that you are the offspring?'

'Not in so many words, but the evidence is irrefutable. Look at the facts. She named me Ernest when I was born. Mother and Hemingway were in Hong Kong at the same time. She was forced to leave the convent when they discovered her pregnancy. Her lips remained sealed for the rest of her life and she never told anyone who my father was. But look at me!' He thumped his chest. 'You can see the family resemblance. My God, man, the evidence is practically prima facie. And most important of all, when I put all the facts together and presented them to her, Mother just smiled enigmatically and never denied it.'

So be it, Lyon thought. Men have died for lesser truths. 'I suppose it's all harmless,' he said.

31

'What do you mean harmless! Damn it, man, not only am I proud of my heritage, but I have always acted with grace under adversity. In addition to that, like any true man, I've got the proper cojones.' He paused in his tirade and lowered his voice. 'Have I mentioned this to you before?'

'Oh, possibly you've made some brief allusions, a hint here, a sprig of suspicion there.'

'The Hemingway family has never recognized me, of course. But I know my heritage and I've spent the majority of my adult life dedicated to the study of my father's work.'

'Some people consider your book, *Machismo*, a benchmark in American literary criticism,' Lyon said.

'You wouldn't know that from reading the crappy articles Morgan writes. That junk he published in *New Forward* really got to me. "Bloody Rights or Bloody Rites." If the goddamn Brotherhood of Beelzebub hadn't vowed to get him, I might have contracted a hit myself. I probably should have gone ahead and made arrangements as job insurance, since the bastard is never going to give me that endowed chair.'

'Morgan doesn't have the final word on that, you know,' Lyon said. 'The department head only recommends, and the full faculty council has to vote.'

'There are only two of us in the department who have published enough to be really eligible. And no one in their right mind would vote the chair to Garth Wilkins.'

'That might depend on literary taste,' Lyon said. 'And whether or not you preferred writers like Tennessee Williams and Truman Capote. His book, *The Gentle Americans*, was well received in the academic community.'

'His writers are a bunch of pantywaist scribblers! It's a wonder that a bunch of limp wrists like that could hold pens long enough to create anything.'

'I agree that they are quite a contrast to your machismo group of Hemingway, James Jones, and Norman Mailer.'

'Some men have true cojones, and others . . .' He broke off the sentence to watch a bright yellow Ford Escort slowly proceed up the drive and park carefully behind the RV. The driver was a tall man of an incongruous size for the small car. He unwound from the front seat and hesitantly approached the RV. Garth Wilkins had a narrow cadaverous head which was in direct proportion to the rest of his lanky frame. His height created the impression that he was barely in control of his physical movements, as if he had to constantly wage battle to force his limbs to obey mental commands. He knocked softly on the RV door.

'Some men don't seem to have any,' Ernest said as a completion of his thought. 'Like Garth over there, who's not about to attract anyone's attention with his timid taps.' He flipped a contemptuous finger gesture in the direction of his competitor.

Lyon's front chair legs clanked as he rocked forward and turned to watch the tall man knocking on the metal door. 'Over here!' he called out.

Garth stepped back from the door, gave it a last wistful look, and started up to the patio. 'Are you sure he's in there?'

'I saw him go in this morning after we had breakfast,' Lyon said. 'Are you two speaking?'

'Unfortunately I can't avoid having to speak with Morgan,' Garth said.

'I mean you two,' Lyon said as he gestured toward Ernest, who maintained his back to them as he resumed his pose at the wall.

'Only one of us is going to get that endowed chair,' Garth said. 'And if that poseur should be selected, I will immediately resign from the university.'

'The Gay Alliance will be devastated,' Ernest snorted.

Garth ignored the remark and went through the French doors to the bar cart, where he poured a pony of Dry Sack sherry and one of brandy. He handed Lyon the sherry and sipped on the remaining pony. 'Most psychiatrists feel that extreme homophobic reactions are indicative of severe inner conflicts over sexual identity.'

'Jesus, what bilge water!' Ernest pulled on his drink as if the amount consumed established a certain benchmark of masculinity.

'I wish you were back in the department, Lyon,' Garth said. 'While you were around, at least there was one person who brought some sanity to faculty meetings. I sometimes feel that Morgan backs dissension. One week he'll back me on a question and the next he'll be in the camp of the great white hunter over there.' He shrugged a shoulder toward the man by the wall.

'He not only encourages trouble, he precipitates it,' Ernest said without turning from his mental emplacement of gun positions across the river. 'That's how he gets his jollies. What's the gen, for Christ's sake? Why is he hiding in his tin can? He's the one who invited us out here for a discussion of the vacant chair.'

'He's working on a new literary pastiche for the journal,' Garth said. 'This one really strips Papa naked. I believe he calls it "The Moveable Beast". I understand it's a very funny piece written in an exact replica of the Hemingway style. You know the formula. It's filled with lots of "It was good", and "the wine was cold". The juices run a lot and everyone including the women have mucho cojones.'

'That's it!' Ernest said menacingly. He advanced toward the other teacher until Lyon inserted himself between them and steered Ernest through the French doors.

'Time for a refill,' Lyon said as he escorted him into the living room.

The bearded man began to mix a huge drink. 'I'd appreciate it if you kept confidential the discussion we had before Tinkerbell arrived.'

Garth had stretched out along the top of the stone parapet. 'I do hope your tête-a-tête wasn't about being the bastard son of a certain Nobel winning author.'

Ernest stopped pouring. 'Where did you hear that?'

'For God's sake, Ernest! You've been using that Hemingway's bastard bit to hit on every pretty grad student we've had for the past five years. I've often wondered if it ever worked.'

'I've had my share of conquests.'

'They don't give points for misfires.'

'You're taking a header into the river, faggot!' He started for the patio but was stopped by Lyon's reflexive grasp of his shirt tail.

Garth laughed and shook a limp wrist. 'Why don't I just fly across the river and into the trees?'

Rocco Herbert strode around the corner of the house carrying an empty can of spray paint. He shook the can until it rattled and then slammed it down on a glass-topped table. 'OK, who's the joker?'

'Hopefully someone has painted dirty limericks on Morgan's RV,' Garth said.

'How about graffiti on the side of the construction project crane down the road?' Rocco said.

'Illiterate kids,' Ernest said.

'Kids don't write "Abandon hope all ye who enter here" on condominium projects built out in the middle of nowhere. People who live out in the middle of nowhere next to ugly construction projects spray those things,' Rocco said.

'Abandon hope? They could have picked up that little phrase on *Jeopardy*,' Ernest said.

'Not in Latin.'

'They stopped offering Latin in Murphysville High School four years ago,' Lyon said. 'If that's of any help?' He walked to the edge of the patio and stared toward the skeletal iron structure which seemed to sprout a new story each day. The crane was lifting the last of the day's steel up to what was becoming the third-floor frame. 'We fought that project as best we could, but they cheated and sneaked it around us.'

'And that justifies your use of spray paint?' Rocco asked.

'Don't admit another thing, Wentworth,' Garth said. 'Anything you say will be used against you.'

'All condo developers should be castrated,' Ernest added, and for the first time Garth nodded in agreement.

'Last week someone let the air out of a back hoe's tires,' Rocco said.

'That was an ecologically concerned youth,' Lyon answered. 'A family of fox lived on that site before they began blasting. A vodka and tonic, Rocco?'

'Thanks, but I have a man out on sick leave and have to work. The week before that the crane's ladder disappeared.'

'I gave you permission to search my barn,' Lyon said.

'I was afraid of what I might find,' Rocco said. 'Where's Bea? Maybe she can talk some sense into you.'

'She's in Washington for a convention,' Lyon answered, 'and won't be back until late tomorrow.'

'I hope she can talk some sense into you about this,' Rocco said as he stalked back across the lawn toward his cruiser, parked at the construction site.

A whir of electric motors and the clank of metal against metal made them turn toward the RV. The solid door leading into the RV's living quarters slowly opened. The interior of the vehicle was dark, and since it faced away from the late sun, deep shadows fell across the doorway. The door automatically clamped open against the side.

No one emerged from the vehicle.

'Waiting for Morgan's entrance is similar to anticipating the second coming,' Ernest said.

'Who's out there?' A deep bass voice boomed from the darkened interior of the RV.

'Ernest and Garth,' Lyon called back.

'Has the area been swept for intruders?'

'The pickets are out on the flanks and the balloons are doing air surveillance,' Lyon yelled at the motor home. 'The King's Guard have individually sworn personal allegiance, and the food tasters are on standby.'

'You and those court jesters surrounding you have a rotten sense of humor, Wentworth,' Morgan said as he stepped warily out of the RV.

'He really creates a warm feeling of camaraderie around all he touches, doesn't he?' Garth said in a voice too low for Morgan to overhear.

'If you had two dozen room-temperature-IQ fanatics in black hoods pledging your destruction, you'd be rather wary too,' Morgan said as he carefully spun the combination to relock the RV door.

Lyon watched Morgan approach the patio. His former compatriot had aged well physically. He was one of those individuals who, like certain wines or cheese, gained a deeper depth of character with additional layers of time. It was as if it required a certain number of years for him to grow comfortably into his own features. Deep facial marks that had been unbalanced worry creases on a youthful face became deep character lines when flanked by premature white hair and a short goatee. What had been a young man's slight and non-athletic physique became a trim figure when measured against stouter cohorts. Morgan was well aware of the increasing maturation of his looks, and as they coalesced he began to dress dramatically. While others in the academic world often opted for a tweedy comfortable look, Morgan dressed formally and conservatively in dark hues. His clothes, purchased during biannual trips to London, would have been stylish at a Mayfair high tea. The total physical effect he conveyed culminated in a deep resonant voice inherited from Welsh forebears.

The day's last sun splashed paths of light across the valley and ran bright color spectrums along the surface of the river. The total effect was an eerie Goyaesque landscape of tilted hills, fields and water. Morgan turned away from the view.

'All of this unbridled nature is underwhelming, Wentworth.'

'I'll ask God for a change of venue, Morgan.' Lyon smiled. 'What can I get you to drink?'

'These days I never drink from opened containers, so that rather limits my choice. If the seal is unbroken, a taste of Pernod would be adequate.'

'I guarantee the Pernod is unopened,' Lyon said as he stepped over to the bar cart.

When he was served, Morgan sat at the glass-topped table facing Garth and Ernest, and looked over the narrow rim of his pony as he delicately sipped the Pernod. His two subordinates shifted nervously by the parapet. 'I thought we should meet on neutral ground. Since Wentworth was once a member of our department and is now a university trustee, he understands our goals and problems. This house is a logical place to settle our differences. Even if the location does somewhat resemble a buzzard's aerie.'

Lyon choked on his sherry. 'I thought this was the endowed-chair problem, not a bird watch.'

'In a manner of speaking, but it also involves the whole

future direction of the department,' Morgan said. 'Your book, *The Gentle Americans*, was an attempt, Garth, but flawed. Let's face it, Tennessee wrote the same play seventy-two times. Ernest's *Machismo* has some qualities, but as far as Hemingway is concerned, let us say he is extremely easy to satirize, because he wrote with a big fat phallic Crayola.'

'Are you trying to tell us something, Morgan?' Ernest asked.

'I have asked Thomas at Yale to accept the Ashley chair,' Morgan said.

'That's not right!' Garth said in a strangled voice. 'Thomas is a deconstructionist!'

'I can't believe what I'm hearing,' Ernest Harnell said.

'You two forced me into this position with your constant bickering,' Morgan said. 'If I appoint either one of you, the other would be most unhappy and even more disruptive than you are now. And besides, you are both traditional. It's about time we joined the twenty-first century, and took a modern approach to literary criticism. Both of you are fighting age-old battles that were abandoned long ago. In Thomas we get a strong man from an excellent university with a voluminous publication history. Actually, you should both be grateful that the department has taken this stance.'

'You're a sadistic son-of-a-bitch, Morgan,' Ernest said.

'You've set us both up,' Garth added. 'You played one against the other while never intending to make it a true contest. You didn't play fair with us.'

Morgan smiled. 'Is that right? Fair is what I say it is. You two seem to have forgotten that I'm the one who makes up the rules.'

Five

'Where did you find the sword?' Rocco asked as they entered the stand of pine trees.

Lyon pointed to a spot a dozen feet back from the cliff. 'Over there. I woke up just about where I'm standing now.'

'I don't see any blood on the ground,' Rocco said. 'Strange.'

Lyon shivered as if a cold wind that reeked of must and decay had blown in from a distant place.

Halfway back to the house, Rocco abruptly halted. He pointed at his patrol car parked in front of the main entrance. 'Wasn't Morgan's RV about where the police cruiser is now?'

'That's right. And Ernest Harnell's Ford was next.'

'The other cars that arrived later were parked in a line down the drive directly behind the RV?'

'Yes,' Lyon answered.

'Which means that Morgan's vehicle could not have been moved in any direction during the evening without extracting it from that minor traffic jam.' It was a statement and not an assumption. 'And you're sure you saw Morgan close the RV's door and punch numbers into the door's combination box before he came to the patio?'

'Yes, we all saw him do that.'

'An action that would have relocked the door,' Rocco mused. 'Which means that, while you were all on the patio, no one could have sneaked into the RV to wait for Morgan's return. Any intruder would have to posses the combination.'

'Yes,' Lyon agreed as they continued toward the house.

'If we assume that possibly you didn't knock Morgan off with Excalibur, we seem to already have at least two other suspects.'

'Garth and Ernest?'

'Yes, although it's difficult to believe that someone who could write *The Gentle Americans* could murder someone with a cleaver that size. I'd put Garth down for poison, Derringer or stiletto, but it boggles the mind to picture him waving around an instrument as destructive and bloody as a broadsword.'

'Garth can turn his personality around according to the way he reads the circumstances. I've seen him do it count-less times. He'll exhibit a certain behavior with me or in a classroom, and then he pushes some sort of mental button to turn himself "on" when he wants to provoke Ernest. I wouldn't make that sort of generalization about the man, Rocco. The appearances are deceiving. During the last war, Garth served as a platoon leader in a rifle company for the First Cav. He won a Purple Heart and Bronze Star and finished his tour as a first lieutenant commanding his company.'

'And Ernest was leader of an A team in the Green Berets?'

'Actually, Ernest was a corporal who taught typing at Fort Benjamin Harrison. I believe that's in Indiana.'

Rocco laughed. 'It would seem as if cojones are not all that transferable,' he said as they entered the house.

Bea sat stiffly on the couch in the living room. She looked up from leafing through a *New Yorker* magazine. 'Well?'

'What I don't understand,' Rocco said, 'is why someone didn't obliterate Morgan years ago? Our victim does not sound like an endearing person. Why did you invite him to your house under any circumstance? Did he have any friends or admirers?'

'He was the best teacher I ever knew,' Bea said defen-sively.

'I agree,' Lyon said. 'Morgan may have had definite social lacks, but he was a superb teacher. He was one of the few department chairmen I know of who insisted on teaching a section of freshmen in an English survey course. He had a rare talent in his ability to reach out and encourage young men and women. He had a true calling that took great energy. Perhaps that was the reason for his problems with others. His teaching ground up every available particle of compassion that he possessed. Because those qualities are now gone, we are all diminished by his loss.'

'Morgan had the ability to alienate anyone he wanted. He could be ruthless to young teachers,' Bea said. 'But sometimes in life you accumulate certain people along the way and they become part of your fabric of living.'

Rocco nodded. 'I have a few friends like that. Anything else from last night's events that's germane?' he asked.

'Appetizers and another drink seemed to calm them down a bit,' Lyon said. 'I was still trying to smooth things over when the twins arrived. Rina and Clay Dickensen are Morgan's younger half-brother and sister. Clay's my accountant and had stopped over to do some tax work for me. Rina's newest boyfriend, Skee Chickering, was with them. I suppose you could say that the second half of the party began with the eagle sighting. Or at least when someone thought they saw an eagle. Well, perhaps it was when someone wanted to see an eagle . . .'

'I see one!' Rina screeched in a high-pitched voice that teetered on the cusp of hysteria. 'He's up there! Oh, God, my eagle!' She climbed on the patio parapet and stretched her arms overhead in a gigantic embrace. 'Oh, mighty winged creature, soar high above us and cast down your regal benediction.' She reached for the hand of a muscular man with white-blond hair and the light complexion of a near albino. 'Help me with this.'

Skee chanted what seemed to be a rather garbled mantra as he climbed to the wall next to her. He stood with his feet planted securely apart and grasped her waist with both hands. With flexed knees he hoisted her overhead.

Rina Dickensen's peasant skirt billowed around her hips as she balanced horizontally above Skee's head. She arched her back and extended her arms in a wing-like imitation of flight. He slowly turned her until she faced out over the valley high above the Connecticut River. Her perfectly balanced body seemed poised for a momentary flight over the hills.

It occurred to Lyon that Rina's pose was identical to the

earlier flying configurations assumed by his Wobblies. The similarity between monster and woman stopped with the positioning of their bodies. His benignly ugly Wobblies were neuter, while the lithe person bracketed against the night was definitely a vibrant woman. Her body, outlined clearly against the sky, exuded an animal sensuality.

Rina had the slender taut figure of the gymnast, with the firm hips and buttocks of the trained athlete. The brisk river wind swirled her clothing to reveal long legs, while its slight chill through the thin material of her blouse stiffened her nipples. Her presence disturbed Lyon, not because of her bizarre exhibitionism, but because he suspected that the real reason for the taunting exposure was a seductive game that she persisted in playing. He wasn't able to measure the seriousness of her intent, and wasn't about to explore it further.

Skee slowly shifted position on the parapet. He turned in a half circle until Rina's head pointed directly toward the house, where Lyon stood framed in the window of his study. She smiled. Her lips mouthed words lost in the wind. Skee shifted position again as he slowly lowered her to the ground. She slid from his arms and performed a perfectly executed back flip culminating in a dexterous curtsey in Lyon's direction. They gave her a polite smattering of applause.

'That performance was nearly as good as the day I ran with the bulls in Pamplona,' Ernest said.

'One does not run with the beasts,' Garth said. 'It's corrida de toros.'

Rina's eyes locked with Lyon's until her companion grasped her elbow and steered her toward the far end of the patio.

'Your sister reminds me of a gypsy,' Lyon said to the man intently bent over the computer on his desk. 'She has a certain wild elan about her.'

'Change that to uncontrolled lust for eagles, men and money, not necessarily in that order. Although a rich man who donated to her Eagle Foundation might head the list.'

'Her new boyfriend has money?'

'Whatever Skee has besides muscles, it's certainly not money, but I'm not about to ask Rina what it is.'

Clay Dickensen, working at Lyon's desk, had the hair and skin coloring of his fraternal twin. Brother and sister had the identical shade of black hair that appeared a darker hue when contrasted against their alabaster skin. That combination accentuated their sensual features. Their builds were also similar, although the primary differentiating characteristic was Clay's serious and nearly perpetual half frown, as contrasted against her uninhibited openness.

Lyon sank into the worn leather chair behind the desk and sipped on his sherry. 'How bad is it?'

Clay thumped the thin pile of records by the computer. 'Rotten and lousy!' he said as he swivelled the chair to face Lyon. 'Your financial records are a travesty. I'm going to have to do a lot of interpolating, since I can't ask the IRS for another extension.'

'Interpolation sounds like accountant talk for guessing.'

'It's also secret CPA code that means, I hope to God you don't get audited.'

'I don't want to cheat.'

'With the condition of your records, even strict honesty is going to look suspicious.' He bent over the keyboard with a deepening of his usual frown. 'If you had only kept a travel diary like I suggested last year. I could have given you a hell of a lot more legitimate travel deductions.'

'I tried it,' Lyon said.

'I know,' Clay replied. 'I read it. The first two entries were terrific. You had dates, exact amounts for train fares, taxis, and the lunch with your publisher, all duly noted. Then I got to page three, which turned into a long description of two Wobbly monsters riding the roof of an Amtrack train as it struggled back to Connecticut in a snow storm.'

'Who's Rina's new beau?' Lyon asked in an attempt to divert talk away from his tax problems.

'Skee Chickering is an appropriate addition to my sister's gypsy caravan. He's not only a professional bodybuilder, but is now her business partner in a fitness studio. She leads the acrobatic classes while he instructs on the machines, power-lifting, and tends the juice bar while she goes eagle watching.'

Lyon laughed. 'I don't know if it's due to her interest or

43

not, but the bald eagles are returning to the river valley.'

Clay turned his chair at an angle that allowed him to simultaneously see Rina on the patio and Lyon in the leather chair. 'I shouldn't bad-mouth Skee. He's the one who's gotten her into the health business, and that's a relief from past obsessions with a certain rock band.'

'She seems to be the type of individual who's extremely enthusiastic about everything she does.' Lyon watched Rina suck on an orange with gusto and then throw back her head to laugh at Garth's quip. It was impossible not to notice the way a patio lantern backlit her figure. He realized that Clay was watching him with his usual half frown and he quickly poured another sherry.

'She's always had a crush on you,' Clay said.

'Hey, I'm a happily married guy,' Lyon said.

'You forget that Rina is an aging flower child. The fact that you're married doesn't concern her in the least. She believes in what she calls the full and natural expression of feelings. You and I might call it sexual license. I've never been quite sure if this philosophy is based on some sort of Zen or the residue of too many past drugs. In addition to her girlhood crush on you, I think that she's really got her heart set on the house. She considers Nutmeg Hill as the best location on the river for an eagle sanctuary.'

'Bea and I would never sell this place.'

'Rina knows that. Bea has already told her.'

'I hope you're not suggesting anything. I have no intention of sharing my house with very large feathered friends. And other alternatives won't work, since I'm too old for her,' Lyon said with what he hoped was a note of finality.

'Nothing is too good for the eagles. There is no sacrifice too extreme, although Skee seems to be helping to relieve some of that obsessive pressure. Our older brother doesn't understand that. Morgan still holds it against Rina for dropping out of college in her junior year. It drove him up the wall when she followed the Grateful Dead for fifteen months as a Dead Head.'

'I'm surprised he didn't try and stop her,' Lyon said.

'Oh, but he did. Big brother turned off the money spigot.'

'How could he do that?'

'Although Morgan is only our half-brother, he is the one in charge of the trust our grandparents established. He has so much control that when Rina left college he was able to stop half her money.'

'Morgan's an academic,' Lyon said. 'That breed believes that dropping out of college is the equivalent of deserting an army under enemy fire.'

Clay clicked off the laptop and carefully placed the slim batch of financial records in a file folder. 'The situation got worse. He finally caught up with her at a Dead concert in Foxboro, Massachusetts. There was enough marijuana smoke hovering over the stadium to fog-in an airport. As usual, Rina was exuberantly participating in the festivities. She was wearing a pair of skimpy denim shorts and no top while she sat on some guy's shoulders and screamed and waved her arms every time Garcia plucked a note. Needless to say, Morgan was not amused. That's when he stopped the other half of her trust payments.'

'I'm surprised he has that sort of absolute power under the trust once you reached your majority,' Lyon said.

'I know. It's illogical, but that's how it was set up. His control doesn't end until he decides that we are able to watch over our own affairs. Then he will make final distribution of the principle. When he cut Rina off after the Dead concert, he began to apply financial pressure on me. I was in the midst of studying for my CPA exam when he lowered the boom. He took the position that I was required to bring peer pressure down on Rina. Twin pressure was the exact phrase he used. I was to wrench her away from the arms of the Grateful Dead, detox her from drugs, and turn off her sexual engine. It was just about this time that she discovered eagles. Birds, not the group. Since birds don't seem to thrive at rock concerts and you don't see many zonked bird-watchers, it seemed like a healthy outlet to me. It worked in a way. She traded one obsession for another. She swapped the music for bodybuilding and eagles. The sex stayed.'

'Do I detect a little bitterness here?' Lyon asked.

'Hell, yes! We both resent our pompous half-brother

45

making decisions concerning our lifestyles. He decides what is permissible and punishes us financially if we defy him. Our granddaddy who set the terms of the trust should be dug up and a stake pounded through his heart. We'd both sell our souls to be out from under Morgan.'

'And Rina feels the same?'

'Jesus, yes! Don't get her started on the subject. The only reason she's here tonight is to help me force Morgan to set the exact date for the financial distribution.'

'Rina's not a Dead Head anymore, she's creating a successful business, and her work with an endangered species is certainly a positive step. What reasons does Morgan give for not making the distribution?'

Clay stared intently out the window as if answers floated in the reflections mirrored there. 'I tried to resolve that last month. He told me that I still wore brown shoes and Rina had gone to the birds. Brown shoes and eagles were the obstacles to our getting the money.'

'I don't understand that non sequitur,' Lyon said.

'Morgan insists that there are certain kinds of anal retentive people who wear brown shoes after five at night. Since I fall into that category, I am pegged as retentive. It is his responsibility to me and the trust to change my personality so that I stop hoarding feces, bank accounts and IRS receipts.'

'In other words,' Lyon said. 'The problem in Morgan's eyes is that your sister wants to give her money to an endangered species, and you don't want to spend any of yours?'

'You got it. When I hear contradictions like that, my accountant's mind rings an alarm,' Clay said.

'Have you tried discussing this with him?'

'Come on, Lyon. You know what a pompous ass he is. You don't discuss with big brother. He allows you an opinion as long as it doesn't disagree with his authoritative decree. His democracy gives Rina and me one vote to his six.'

Lyon laughed. 'That's just about how he runs the English department at the university.'

'He's gone too far this time,' the accountant said. 'The situation has reached such serious dimensions that I'm afraid something violent could happen.'

46

Lyon tried to manufacture a reassuring smile, but was afraid that it probably appeared more of a grimace. 'Garth and Ernest may exhibit a lot of bluster and spout words, but they've fought each other and Morgan for years. They are upset right now over a new man coming into the department, but I don't think that they would do anything violent to your brother.'

Clay laughed. 'If they don't get him, there's another candidate in my sister and that muscle-bound hunk she shares her cave with. Skee will do anything Rina tells him, and I'm worried about what she might be whispering in his ear recently.'

'New England families have argued over trust funds for generations,' Lyon said. 'If even a small percentage of those fights ended in mayhem, our cemeteries would be overflowing.'

'The money in the trust was nurtured for two centuries. Sea captains chased whale or sailed two-year trips on the China Run. When the manufacturing age began, they invested in the mills. Now, our half-brother is involved in the worst possible New England sin.' His voice lowered to a hoarse tone that signified his desperation. 'Morgan is dipping into capital.'

Lyon recognized his alarm. Capital depletion was a gross violation of the New England puritan ethic. Profligate spending transcended ordinary sins and other high crimes and misdemeanors. 'Morgan has an excellent salary from the university,' he said in defense of his former teaching mate.

'As a full professor and chair he's drawing eighty-five thousand dollars and you can add another fifty from the trust fund. Deduct a proper per cent for federal and state income taxes for that bracket and he's taking home. . .' He punched some numbers into a small pocket calculator. 'Exactly eighty-nine K a year.'

'Some people manage to somehow squeak a living from that sort of money, Clay.'

'I know the man's lifestyle. He makes at least two trips a year to the continent on Concorde. He stays at the Savoy in London, and buys suits and accessories from the best tailors on Bond Street. That tank he has parked in your driveway set him back a hundred thou after he finished redoing it. Add these little items to the cost of his wine cellar, the bimbo he keeps in Boston, and you find that the man is living at a standard that calls for two, two point five a year. He's making up that shortfall with our money!'

'That's supposition,' Lyon said. 'He sells articles to those journals.'

Clay snorted. 'They pay peanuts.'

'Clay's right. He's taken our money,' Rina said from the doorway.

As both men turned to look at her, she automatically assumed a pose against the doorframe. She leaned her shoulders back and thrust her hips forward. She slowly waved a large glass of papaya juice in their direction. Lyon wasn't sure what signal this posture was supposed to transmit, but it seemed to fall somewhere between wanton sexuality and 'screw you guys for all I care'. He was struck again with the strong resemblance between the brother and sister.

'Are you still ready to beard the bastard tonight, Clay?' she continued.

'I told him yesterday that I'd be at Nutmeg Hill tonight to work on Lyon's taxes. I also said I would ask you to come so we could talk about a final accounting of the trust.'

'What was his answer after he finished laughing?' Rina asked.

'There wasn't any answer, just one of his *will you now*s.'

Rina turned toward Lyon with a vehemence. 'I need that money. Skee and I have entered into a franchise agreement with a national health club and we're obligated to open two more outlets in a sixty-day period. That takes start-up money. I have also promised the Eagle Foundation a sizable donation to continue the good results we're seeing with the arrival of new birds in the area. I want my damn capital now!'

'Bravo, my eaglet!' Morgan's resonant bass voice reverberated through the study. He pushed into the room and seemed to occupy its full dimensions by the power of his personality. 'Aren't they a sterling pair, Lyon?' he said with an expansive gesture toward his half-siblings. 'The feminine part of one end of our gene pool thinks she is a bird. The male portion of the pair, such as it is, has a bookkeeper mind of dimensions so broad that it staggers the imagination of Lilliputians.'

'Knock it off, Morgan,' Clay said. 'We're here to talk money.'

'Aren't you always, you minion of the tax authorities? Did it ever occur to you that the principle you're so worried about might have been added to by my small efforts in real estate and the stock market?'

'That possibility never crossed my mind,' Clay answered.

'The only thing you've added is bastards in Boston,' Rina said.

'You are both bloodsucking leeches who don't deserve or know how to properly benefit from money,' Morgan said.

'Deserve is not the point, Morgan,' Clay said with resignation.

Morgan shifted his venom toward Rina. 'While you salivate over this money, did it ever occur to your uneducated mind that the trust is tainted? It's money that originated with the slave trade. Yankee skippers who didn't make the China Run. They converted to the triangle trade with vessels that considered the loss of one third the human cargo as a normal cost of doing business. After that practice was outlawed, they turned to the mills. These were the gallant establishments that tallied small fortunes through the exploitation of very young women and children. The mills moved south to exploit others, and our forefathers found an even better source of profit in the weapons of death. Connecticut, the arsenal of the world, the manufacturers of every lethal weapon known to man, from atomic submarines to most of the handguns sold in this country. But that was all yesterday, you say. Today the money is invested in squeaky-clean stocks and bonds. Our assets have been properly laundered, as old money should be.'

'You seem to have enjoyed its pleasures without guilt,' Clay said. 'Frankly, Morgan, we are not interested in your financial philosophy. I want an immediate accounting of our money.'

49

'And your sister's share will either be wasted on that muscle-bound jerk she's sleeping with or bird-watching old ladies in tennis shoes.' Morgan turned to Lyon. 'Her newest is a real Neanderthal, Lyon. I think she discovered him when she tripped over a rock on Muscle Beach and found him underneath.'

Lyon felt that this family argument was violating the sanctuary he had tried to create in his small office. The room had turned from a quiet place for thought and creativity to a pocked battlefield of age-old bitterness.

'Cut the crap, Morgan!' Rina said. 'I want my money.'

'If there's any left,' Clay added in a low voice.

'I won't even deign to answer that,' Morgan said as he strode from the room.

'It's time for action, Rina,' Clay said.

'I agree,' she replied.

The subdued group filed back to the patio. Lyon was concerned over the dysfunctional family scene he had just witnessed. Morgan's imperious attitude was creating a deep anger in the twins that might be impossible to rectify.

The phone rang as he passed the kitchen doorway. He reached toward the wall unit and flipped it off its stanchion. 'Wentworth here,' Lyon said.

'Tell Mr Morgan that Armageddon has begun,' the flat nasal voice said.

Six

Lyon paced the living room. With complete absorption in the act, he strode in a perfect box pattern as if he were taking measured steps to produce room dimensions. 'All right,' he finally said. 'It would seem that our primary suspects are two disgruntled English teachers, and a set of mismatched twins agitated over their trust fund.'

'The threatening phone call talked of Armageddon,' Rocco said. 'It wasn't a call from some kids asking us to let Prince Albert out of the box.'

'Is there more?' Bea asked.

'Yes,' Lyon answered.

'What's Armageddon?' Rina asked.

'Why, my dear sister,' Morgan's voice boomed over the patio. 'Your experience with that rock group certainly left some lacunae in your education. Perhaps Mr Wentworth has a large dictionary in the house that he can teach you to use.'

'The final battle between the forces of good and evil,' Lyon said.

'Designed to take out Morgan?' Rina asked.

'It would seem so,' Lyon answered.

'Fanaticism can't be all that bad,' Clay mumbled.

'You know, I heard that,' Morgan said. 'The only principle your accountant's brain ever comprehended was a lowering of the capital gains tax.'

'I don't screw people over,' Clay retorted.

'I don't need this!' Morgan said. 'Good night.' He strode off the patio toward his RV.

'Wait a minute!' Clay yelled after him. 'We haven't settled anything.'

51

Morgan ignored the comment as he violently punched numbers into the door's lock combination.

'Stop him,' Rina said in a husky voice.

Skee jumped off the patio steps and sprinted down the drive. He reached the RV at the moment the door swung open and Morgan stepped inside. The bodybuilder caught the edge of the door before it slammed shut. He jerked the other man into the doorway. 'Rina wants you, Daddio.'

Morgan shoved Skee's hand off his shoulder and reached back inside the van to produce a long broadsword. He raised the weapon over his head with both hands. 'You move. You even breathe,' he said, 'and I will separate that notochord you call a brain from your long neck.'

'I wouldn't make book that he won't,' Clay said to Rina. 'You had better call Muscles off.'

'Leave him alone,' Rina commanded.

Skee Chickering backed away from the glinting sword. When he was out of its thrusting reach he turned and walked nonchalantly back to the patio. Morgan continued standing in front of the RV door with the sword until Skee sat at a patio table. He slowly lowered the weapon and stepped back inside the van and slammed the door.

'Does he always wave that thing around?' Skee asked no one in particular.

'He has two,' Garth said. 'He used to keep them both in his office, where they hung on the wall. They're props for a course he teaches in Arthurian legends.'

'Old English legends, like in Spenser's *Faerie Queen*,' Ernest said pointedly to Garth.

'Who says that's Arthurian?' Garth retorted.

The clank of heavy metal shutters caused them to turn toward the van. The final metal plate closed off the last window, and only a rim of gold light could be seen around the window borders.

After they finished eating, Lyon arranged a rare steak on a hot platter, surrounded by thick fries, salad and garlic bread. He carried the portion waiter-style at shoulder height down the drive to Morgan's RV. He knocked on the heavy metal door three times before a muffled growl issued from the interior.

'Who the hell is it?'

'Wentworth, Morgan. I brought you a steak with fixings.'

'Give it to Rina's animal. His appetite for red meat is undoubtedly immense. No prepared meals, Wentworth. I am surrounded by my enemies and contamination of my food would not be beyond their addled senses. When I am hungry I shall prepare my own meal from unopened containers untouched by human hands.'

'Suit yourself,' Lyon said. The man's paranoia was reaching a critical stage. He returned to the patio and handed the warm steak to Skee. Morgan was right. Without acknowledging the appearance of the additional food, the bodybuilder immediately dedicated himself to its consumption.

Ernest assumed a heroic pose by the parapet. 'I would very much like to have Morgan on safari with me. Accidents can be readily arranged in the bush.'

'In the service we called it fragging,' Garth said. 'Why don't we separate his head from the rest of him with that broadsword he's so enamored with?'

'Certainly not!' Ernest snapped. 'That hunk of iron is awkward and devoid of grace. If there's any Morgan-sticking to be done, I would only consider a matador's sword.'

'The estoque,' Lyon said as he stacked plates.

'Yes, of course,' Ernest admitted. 'Educated cojones,' he said admiringly of Lyon as he searched for his car keys. Still cloaked by their mutual anger at Morgan, both teachers returned to their cars. They only managed a brief argument over who would back down the drive first.

'We're going to have to hire a lawyer to bring an action against Morgan,' Rina said.

Clay nodded. 'I hate to wash dirty family laundry in public, but I don't know what else we can do to force him to make the trust distribution.'

'I broke the fingers of the last guy who threw down on me with a weapon,' Skee Chickering said.

'What a magnificent aerie this property would make,' Rina said with passion. She stood on the parapet for the second time and made a broad sweeping gesture over the night. 'Eagles would command the river valley from here to the

Sound. Nests would proliferate and the young would be raised and taught the ways of the bird.'

'Are we to share Nutmeg Hill with your flock?' Lyon asked.

'You don't seem to understand that these aren't ordinary birds, Lyon,' Clay said. 'We do not speak of them as feathered creatures like Tweety in a cage or little robin redbreast hopping around after worms. They are always referred to as THE EAGLES. It is generally considered good form if you use some powerful adjectives such as magnificent, soaring winged creatures.'

'We can drop the sarcasm, dear brother,' Rina said as she climbed down from the wall and handed her empty juice glass to Skee for a refill. 'As soon as I get my trust money, I will make an offer on this place,' she said to Lyon.

Lyon shook his head. 'Sorry, Rina. We have no plans to sell.'

'Everyone has a price,' Skee said.

After they left, it took Lyon over an hour to straighten the patio and kitchen. He loaded the dishwasher, flicked it on and made a final patio check before throwing the switch to douse the exterior lights. As the patio floods clicked off, he thought he glimpsed movement in the periphery of his vision. He quickly turned off the living-room lights and stepped back into the shadows to let his eyes accommodate to the dark.

He knew that night vision was initially more effective if you viewed an object obliquely rather than look at it directly. He tilted his head to see out of the corner of his eyes. He thought he saw movement in the shadows beyond the house. A low bush brushed by the wind could be deceiving. It would be impossible to discern shadows properly until his eyes gained their night vision. The outside world appeared as a slab of darkness until scudding clouds moved on and a half moon crept out. He felt his way through the darkened house to the closet by the front door. On the upper shelf was a powerful five-battery lantern that cast a wide beam.

There were now faint sounds nearer the house. He heard two quick steps in the gravel as someone crossed from one side of the drive to the other.

Under ordinary circumstances he would have called out and turned on the floods mounted on the corners of the house and over the patio. Morgan's presence in the RV parked in the drive radically changed those circumstances. The phone threats couldn't be discounted. Morgan might be safe in his armored vehicle, but since terrorists didn't seem to differentiate between the innocent and guilty, they could all be in harm's way.

There were more steps in the drive near Morgan's vehicle, followed by an odd clicking sound. The passing minutes had allowed Lyon time to obtain part of his night vision. He slipped through the French doors, carrying the lantern.

He pressed against the house wall to take advantage of their deep shadows and slowly worked his way down the steps and around the corner of the building.

The nearer he got to the RV, the clearer the persistent clicking sounds. He paused in the remaining shadows at the far corner of the house and was able to identify the clicks. Someone was punching numbers into the door's combination panel. When one series didn't work, they tried again with a different grouping.

He knelt before he clicked on the flashlight. 'Don't move! I have a weapon!'

She gave a startled gasp and then turned to throw up her arms as if to shield herself from the shot. She squinted into the light that shone directly in her face. 'Is that you, Bear Baby? It's about time.'

'Who are you?'

'A friend of Morgan's,' she said.

Lyon wondered if the shrinking contingent of Morgan's friends might not be an endangered species more vulnerable than spotted owls and snow leopards. 'Do you usually creep around people's lawns in the middle of the night attempting to break into motor homes?'

'The bastard changed the combination on me.' She turned to pound on the door with her fist. 'Morgan! I know you can hear me. Open up, Morgan! It's me, Bambi.'

Lyon cringed. He knew that people were actually named

55

Bambi, and wondered if Thumper and Flower were far behind. 'How did you get out here?'

'Why? Do I get to play twenty questions with you?'

'Yes, you do, because this is my property and you are trespassing.'

'So, I got confused over directions and cut the turn into this place too tight. My pickup slid into the culvert down by the road.' She resumed thumping on the heavy metal door with both fists. 'Morgan! Damn it! Open the frigging door.'

She was a voluptuous woman wearing sneakers and tight designer jeans that stretched tautly across her rump. A white shirt, open one button too far, covered large and impossibly pointed breasts. Her full figure was topped with a huge mass of flaming auburn hair that Lyon suspected was not its original color, since he had never seen that particular shade of red before. The harsh light of the powerful lamp revealed somewhat coarse features with lines around the eyes that signified more years than her figure seemed to suggest.

She turned her anger toward Lyon. 'That son-of-a-bitch has no intention of opening the door. So, what are you going to do about it, Wimp Face?'

Lyon laughed. 'Wimp Face is not going to do anything about it.'

She pointed to the large lantern which dangled from his hand. 'Were you really going to shoot me with that flashlight?'

'Actually, I have never heard of any terrorists named Bambi. Do you have a full name or don't creatures of the wood need one?'

Part of her tension dissipated and she nearly smiled at him. 'It's Bambi Dolores. That's my stage name, since I am a dancer.'

'Oh, I see,' he said, to hide more confusion over this late-night visitor. She seemed too large for ballet, a bit too coarse for a theatrical chorus, and somehow he couldn't place her in an interpretive modern dance company.

'That guy really isn't coming out tonight, is he?'

'I would think not,' Lyon answered.

She sighed. 'So that the night is not a complete waste, how about a drink before you help me get my truck out?'

His curiosity was piqued over Morgan's choice of women. This tough redhead standing fearlessly before him did not seem the sort of person the suave Morgan would pursue. 'There's got to be a bottle of something left on the bar cart. Come on up to the house.'

She walked by his side and stared up at the widow's walk that dominated the top of Nutmeg Hill. 'This is some mansion, mister. If this is your place and you aren't just the guy who does the grounds, you must be loaded.'

Lyon laughed at the ingenuousness which seeped around the edge of her tough veneer. 'I'm hardly loaded. It's a big old house, but hardly a mansion. It only has twelve rooms. It looks larger because of the way it's situated on the bluff.' He flipped on the living-room light and went back into the kitchen. He heard her exploring the living room while he shoveled cubes from the refrigerator into the ice bucket. He checked the contents of the bar cart. 'There's some scotch left.' He noticed that one bottle of Dry Sack was empty, and the other had its seal broken. He poured a pony for himself and a Dewars and water for her.

'Hey, that looks like real honest-to-God sipping scotch and not colored water. Hit me again with the good stuff.'

Lyon was beginning to glimpse a possible niche in the dance world that she might inhabit. 'Your accent,' he said, 'sounds like South Boston.'

She drained half her drink. 'You don't win the brass ring for that one. I've got the map of Ireland plastered across my face, and my voice sounds like a Kennedy who never went to school.'

'And you dance in the Combat Zone?'

She appraised him over the rim of her glass before answering. 'Topless at the White Pussy Cat. Morgan's told you about me, huh?' A ribald laugh peeled forth. 'Morg always says I have the upper works of a first-class battleship and the morals of a submarine.' She peered into her drink. 'I've never been quite sure if that's a compliment or not.'

'Obviously he didn't expect you tonight,' Lyon said.

'Oh, he knew I'd arrive eventually. If not tonight, tomorrow or the next day. Recently I've become to Morg, like what do they say? Like a bad penny.' She held out her glass for a refill. 'In the beginning he paid plenty to have me spend a half hour in the sack with him. Not that I'm in the business, Morg was just helping out with the rent. Since the baby came I can't get a word or a buck out of him.'

'Baby?'

'Barney. You know, named after . . .'

'I know.'

'I love you. You love me,' she sang in an off-key voice that cracked when she reached for the higher registers.

Lyon had accidentally viewed TV's ersatz dinosaur twice. On the first occasion he thought the character was a temporary dash of treacly bad taste that would momentarily disappear. He was astonished to rediscover the monster two months later. He was convinced that the beast gave all monsters a bad name and should be immediately eliminated. He supposed it was in the natural order of things that mothers named Bambi had kids named Barney. 'I'm surprised that Morgan's involved in the baby business.'

'You've got his number, Wimpo. He told me a hunret times he hates human life forms under three feet tall who can't read at a college level. Of course, he claims he's not the father, but I know better.'

'They now have genetic tests that can establish parentage definitively,' Lyon said.

'You even talk like him.'

'Once that's established,' Lyon continued, 'you can go through the courts for child support.'

'I want more than a few bucks a week, Wimp Man. The only reason I put one in the oven with Morg was so that the kid could grow up and not be window-lace Irish. Look at me. My Da was a cop and I'm dancing bare boobs at the Pussy Cat so horny guys can slip dollar bills under my G-string. No way is Barney growing up in South Boston. He ain't goin' the way of the other smart Irish micks who drop out of school and snatch cars to order for a hunret a pop.'

'I would think not,' Lyon said, aware that he was now going to get the unabbreviated version of the affair.

She settled expansively back on the couch and took a slow slurp of her drink before she continued. 'In the beginning Morg couldn't get enough of me. It started a couple of years ago when he was in Boston for some academic bash and staying at the Parker House. He got bored one night and dumped the crowd he was with and wandered over to the Pussy Cat. I was doing my mermaid number when he grabbed a stool right in front of me and ordered scotch. Nobody but nobody orders scotch at the Pussy Cat. I knew he was fresh fish, and the scotch bit really slayed me, so I stayed on the ramp right in front of him doing my thing. I mean, I flashed it right at him. Tween turns he bought me a couple of house cocktails, you know, ginger ale calling itself champagne. He kept laughing at me, like everthin' I said was funny. After a couple drinks of that kerosene, he began to stop laughing and looked at me funny. He offered me a couple of big ones to come back to his room. I'm not in the business and don't usually turn tricks, but that week I needed cash for the rent, and so I went. Old Morg seemed to like the merchandise and kept coming back for more. It really turned him on to spend an hour at the bar watching me dance before we went back to his place for a quickie. He began driving up most weekends and musta' spent a fortune at the club, and another one paying my expenses. That's when I decided to get knocked up by the bastard. I figured with a college professor da and the money that Morg said his family had, the kid would be golden.

'When I started showing, I got bounced. I mean, not only didn't I have a job at the Cat anymore, but Morg kissed me off. All of a sudden he doesn't even know my name. The bigger I got, the worse his memory. He don't know my address, and I think he even forgot where Boston was. Well, it's payback time. Barney wants his divvies and I mean to see that he gets them or we'll see who does the final kissing-off.'

She yawned and plunked her empty glass on the cocktail table before stretching. The movement thrust her miraculously shaped bosom forward.

'I'm coming back tomorrow night to camp on his doorstep or running board or whatever,' she continued. 'He's got to come out of that junk heap eventually. Can you give me a hand with my truck? It's a little four by four and I think even you can help me out of the ditch.'

Lyon left the yard floods on to light their way down the drive to its entrance at the highway. Her red pickup was canted into a drainage ditch. He got behind the wheel and rocked it back and forth until the traction spun the wheels off the soft shoulder. They switched places and she drove off with a wave.

A deep weight of fatigue slipped over him as he started back to the house.

Tendrils of ground fog seeped over the promontory, through the stand of pine, and flowed into low ground dips. Two spotlights backlit the widow's walk, casting bizarre shadows across the lawn at his front. The skewered images of the walk's rail made strut shadows appear on the ground as distorted battlements.

Lyon stopped stock still and rubbed his eyes for focus. His body was nearly at the point of exhaustion. His perceptions began to shift toward an aura of unreality. The fifty yards to the house represented an infinite distance that stretched endlessly toward a narrowing horizon. Tree shadows swayed in a macabre dance that appeared vaguely threatening. He felt trapped in a universe he did not comprehend.

Their once familiar house appeared alien. Its new identity exuded a foreboding aura.

He felt light-headed and separated from his body, as if he were floating above the trees in a weightless condition. He somehow sensed that he had to reach the safety of the house for survival.

He was never sure where it came from. It might have been ejected from the house, or propelled out of Morgan's RV, or catapulted shrieking from the dark stand of trees that bordered the lawn. He only knew that the cowled figure rushing toward him carried a raised broadsword in both hands.

Lyon immediately turned and staggered toward the tree line. The apparition behind him, its face cloaked by its hood, lumbered after him with the sword blade making narrow circles in the air.

He reached the tree line and stumbled. The sword swept through the air and bit into a tree trunk inches from his head.

Seven

Chief Rocco Herbert looked extremely unhappy. Bea Wentworth stared off into space with a glazed, fearful look. 'Does anyone buy this?' Rocco asked. 'You can't identify this . . . thing who initiated the assault?'

'No.'

'You seem to be rather successfully framed. You possess the combination into the van, and presumably you were the only one conscious at Nutmeg Hill during the time of the murder. You also had possession of the murder weapon.'

'I told you. I was unconscious for the remainder of the night. After I fell, I passed out so quickly that I'm convinced I was drugged.'

'Possibly something was put in your sherry?'

'That's the first thing I considered. The wine would be the most logical place to dissolve something, since I was the only one drinking Dry Sack.' He gestured toward the bar cart. 'The bottle is missing. There is no way to run a drug screen.'

'When you invited the topless dancer into the house, you left her alone in the living room for several minutes while you went into the kitchen. When you returned you noticed the seal broken on the fresh bottle.'

'She had an opportunity to spike the bottle. It was a crowded evening, so a bunch of other people had plenty of chances to contaminate the liquor.'

'Bambi was the only one who knew you were going to take a drink from that particular bottle at that exact time,' Bea said. 'Since she controlled the conversation, she might have monitored the time it took for the drug's effect.'

'I had never met the woman before,' Lyon said. 'How would she know I drank Dry Sack?'

62

'She was the decoy, obviously,' Bea said. 'You said she drove off in her truck, but shortly after, you were attacked. Partners.'

Rocco nodded in agreement. 'Let's go back to the assault. Surely you can come up with some sort of description of your assailant?'

'No,' Lyon said. 'I can't even tell you if it was a man or woman. She or he was wearing a long robed garment with a wide cowl that completely hid the face.'

'Did the clothing appear to belong to a cult of any kind?'

Lyon shrugged. 'Just as easily that as a monk's habit. I've told you all I can.'

Patrolman Jamie Martin appeared in the doorway. 'There's a call for you on the radio, Chief.'

After Rocco left, Lyon and Bea sat motionless and silent at opposite ends of the room.

'I think you're in big trouble,' Bea finally said.

'I think possibly you're right,' Lyon replied.

They continued their silent vigil without further comment until Rocco returned. A wide grin seemed to have replaced the chief's past skepticism. 'Talk about luck of the damned,' he said. 'They just read me a letter that was hand carried to the station a few minutes ago. If it holds up, everything falls into place.'

'What in the world are you talking about?' Lyon asked.

'Let me read you the damn thing verbatim,' Rocco said as he pulled out his notebook. 'The original is evidently written in a smeary red ink which I suppose is meant to be blood, although I'd put my money on poster paint. The lab can pin that down for us. It reads, "Satan has been gloriously revenged and the first infidel has died in the Armageddon. Thus it is to all those who deny the true magnificence of Satan."'

'That sounds like those Beelzebub guys are taking credit for Morgan's death.'

'It sounds that way to me, unless Armageddon is a new fast-food joint,' Rocco said.

'The consensus from Norbie and the state's attorney is that the hooded figure who attacked Lyon was a member of the sect who threatened Morgan. That attack was due to mistaken identity, and was aborted once they realized he was not their target. Then person or persons unknown somehow obtained the door combination. They entered the vehicle and dispatched Morgan with one of his own swords. The state's attorney is not pursuing a warrant against you, Wentworth. The state police are now directing all their energies toward locating the man or men who performed the killing.'

'Man?' Bea asked with a pronounced question in her voice.

'Fanatics of this type would never allow a woman to perform a ritualistic murder like this,' Lyon said.

'Considering the background of the sect, the zeal with which the killing was performed and the strength required,' Rocco said, 'I think we can assume it was a man.'

'Your pat little exoneration is welcome but it bothers me,' Bea said. 'Suppose whoever drugged and chased after Lyon with the sword was framing him for Morgan's killing. It doesn't make sense that the Beelzebubs would go to that trouble and then turn around and take public credit for the murder.'

'The state has turned its attention elsewhere for the time being,' Rocco said. 'I think you're damn lucky to be off the hook.'

'How do we know it's not a nut letter? That sort of thing happens all the time,' Lyon said.

'We had all best hope that there's some sort of follow-up to make this a permanent suspicion, or Norbie's blinkers will turn back in Lyon's direction. I got to go.'

'Don't look at me,' Lyon said to Bea after Rocco left. 'I have a Wobbly book to finish.'

'My political fences need mending before the nominating convention,' Bea said. 'But somebody killed Morgan right outside our front door.'

'And you're not buying the Armageddon bit?'

Bea looked pensive. 'That's always possible, except that explanation seems to have a lot of loose ends. I should see to the kitchen,' she said.

'I did it last night before the dancer arrived,' he replied.

Bea sighed. 'OK, I have to ask. What happened to my living-room drape?'

'I think that Norbert's men took it as evidence,' Lyon said.

'I hesitate to ask. But why?'

'The blood.'

'On the drape?'

'There was a question of shock. That is, when Rocco thought I was mortally injured, since I was covered with blood.'

'Holding the sword?'

'Yes. He wrapped me in the drape.'

Bea sighed again. 'OK, I asked and you answered. You know, Lyon, sometimes I have the feeling you should never be left alone.'

'I appreciate your trying to take the fall for me on the murder charge,' Lyon said. 'Did you really think that I was capable of killing Morgan? With a huge sword yet?'

She flashed him a smile. 'I walked smack-dab into the middle of a situation without all the facts. The few I did know were pretty darn gloomy. I somehow thought that as a woman I would get less jail time. Last year on one of my senate committees, I toured male and female max security. Believe me, you want female.'

'I suppose there's some sort of weird logic in that,' Lyon said, 'although either of us in the slammer wouldn't do much for the golden years of our marriage.'

Sarge's Bar and Grill was an anachronism that had accommodated to gentrification. The owner, a former army master sergeant, once had a retirement dream of owning a working man's sports bar with a boilermaker clientele who enjoyed betting on an occasional ball game. Initially, its location in an older residential area not far from a ball-bearing factory had guaranteed the right mix of customers. When the factory vacated its building to move to South Carolina and was replaced by a gigantic art gallery, gentrification struck like a thunderclap. The customers were soon divided into two distinct groups. During the day retired workers nursed beers and discussed ball games without wagers. At six the bar's atmosphere radically changed. The night manager arrived with a German chef and a bartender who actually knew how to mix drinks. Cans of Bud mated with cheap house whiskey abdicated to German food served with imported wines and beers placed on checkered tablecloths lit by quaint bottles holding flickering candles.

On most days, Sarge made a valiant and usually successful attempt to drink himself unconscious before the last boiler-maker was chug-a-lugged and the first bottle of Zinfandel was uncorked.

Rocco Herbert was the rare customer who straddled both groups. He qualified as a daylight drinker, and after dusk he often turned into an exuberant sauerbraten customer. Their former military service together required Sarge to maintain a constant supply of properly chilled vodka and ground sirloin for the police chief's gourmet burgers. Lyon was accom-modated by a Dry Sack sherry supply, but like other ordin-ary day customers, any hunger pangs had to be satisfied with pickled eggs or pig's feet.

In his daylight mode, Rocco occupied a booth in the far corner near the window that overlooked a four-way stop sign down the block. Walkie-talkie communication with Jamie Martin's hidden cruiser usually made this observation post a productive spot for generating traffic tickets.

Lyon watched from the bar as a flagrant violator in a green Corvette sped through the stop sign without slowing and then proceeded to swing around a stationary school bus.

Although Rocco was looking directly at the offending vehicle, his hand never toggled the transmission switch of the small radio on the table at his front.

Sarge handed Lyon a sherry and shook his head. 'Captain's not himself these days.'

'How long's he been here?'

'Came in yesterday and back again this morning.'

Lyon carried his drink back to the booth's morose occu-pant. He and Rocco had been friends for many years. Rocco was born and raised in Murphysville and was already chief of police when Lyon and Bea moved to town. The two men had met earlier, during their military service. Rocco, a mustang officer commissioned from the ranks, was a Ranger and commander of the division's reconnaissance platoon.

Lyon, a Yale graduate, was a junior intelligence officer on the staff of Division G-2. He was often thrown in contact with Rocco when the Rangers acted as the division's eyes and ears.

Although both men had been born and raised in the river valley area of Connecticut, it wasn't until the Easter-night ambush that they became friends. Lyon had accompanied the platoon as an observer during a helicopter insertion to locate an enemy battalion. They had come under heavy fire before the helicopters had lifted off. Machine guns with clear fields of fire were emplaced on both sides of the clearing and placed them in a murderous crossfire. The automatic weapons began to methodically rake their positions with devastating results. Lyon knew that it was only a question of minutes until they were damaged sufficiently to be overrun by frontal assault. Rocco, without proper covering fire, had single-handedly flanked one automatic weapon and destroyed it with grenades. He had urged his men into the protecting cover of a nearby bushy draw, where he carried the wounded Lyon. They were removed at dawn, with more than half of Rocco's men killed or wounded.

'Are we home?' Lyon asked as he sipped his sherry. Rocco continued to stare intently at the distant stop sign. 'Catch many today?'

'A few. This case is a real bastard, isn't it?'

'I find it odd that Bambi never came back by my house yesterday or today.'

'The logical answer is that she heard about the murder on TV and went home. It's doubtful she'd come to visit a corpse.'

'A possibility, but she might have stayed around. I think we should find out.'

'It's a big state and she could be anywhere,' Rocco said.

'It's a small state and she could be someplace nearby,' Lyon countered.

'Check out the motels,' Rocco said.

'That's a police function, Chief. You have the staff and contacts to do it faster than I can.'

'Topless with Morgan, it boggles the mind,' Rocco said as he shook his head and slipped from the booth to go to the bar, where he reached under the counter and pulled out a touch-tone phone. He sat on a stool near the beer spigots and punched in numbers.

'Helen, it's the chief. I want you and whoever's holding down communications to do a motel check for me. Lyon Wentworth is with me and will give you the description of the female Caucasian we're looking for. Call me back at Sarge's when you've made the survey.' He handed the phone to Lyon.

'Hi, Helen . . . I'm just fine, and Bea's well. How's Henry? I missed you when I was by the station recently. Right, the description. Her name is Bambi Dolores but that's an alias and she might register under a different name. She's a tall woman with a very full figure. Her age is mid-thirties and she has a distinctive pile of red hair.'

Sarge Renfroe looked up from a sink of soaking glasses. 'I saw her.' He dried his hands on a suspicious-looking bar rag. 'I had to fill in for the evening barman and saw her come in,' he said in his whiskey baritone. 'Ol' Red sidled right up to Clay Dickensen. They seemed to know each other.'

'Oh?' Rocco said. His interest was piqued immediately. 'Tell us more, Sarge.'

'Not much to tell, Captain. Clay was in here drinking a diet coke. You know he don't touch hard stuff. And Red waltzes in here with long legs into next week and hair shaped like a pyramid. She's got front works big enough to pierce a Bradley fighting vehicle. The night manager is having a fit, since he thinks she's imported business wanting to score. But in ten seconds she and Clay are huddled in the corner talking. She knocks down a couple doubles before they leave together.'

'Did they drive off in her truck or Clay's car?' Lyon asked.

'Don't know which one,' Sarge answered, 'but two people left here in one vehicle.'

'What was in the lot when you opened the next morning?' Lyon asked.

The retired master sergeant with the pocked face and bulbous nose thought a moment as he dried his hands again. 'Nuthin'. I remember the lot being empty as Jody's locker.'

'Which means they went off together and someone came back later to pick up a vehicle,' Rocco said.

'Which one?' Lyon wondered.

To get to Clay Dickensen's condominium from Sarge's they had to pass Murphysville Green and go out toward Route 155. Two blocks beyond the center of town they passed a low office building that housed the Clay Dickensen Group, specializing in accounting services and computer technology for small businesses.

Lyon wondered why Clay still retained him as a personal client. The young CPA's firm seemed successful enough that its proprietor did not have to handle individual accounts as unimportant as the Wentworths'. He'd add that question to the lengthening list of items to ask Clay.

The accountant's town house condo was located in a cluster development designed and priced for upscale professionals more concerned over their personal health than propagating the species. Heritage Acres offered every possible recreational facility this section of the country could provide. Grouped around a man-made lake with a small island in the center that housed the kayak house, the project boasted a full-service clubhouse with indoor pool. A complete gym and jogging track were built next to a nine-hole golf course. The open land between building clusters was crisscrossed with landscaped walks, cross-country ski trails, outdoor jogging trails, and interspersed with various types of courts where games with various small rubber balls were played. The area was immaculately maintained through immense monthly charges.

He wondered if there was a pattern between this construction and the condo-monstrosity going up next to Nutmeg Hill. The days when homes were built around schools and playgrounds seemed past. Perhaps the affluent portion of the human race would eventually perish due to the lack of living quarters that permitted children.

Lyon added another mental note to his ever-expanding list of Clay queries. Why was the young CPA so obsessed with the distribution of the trust money when his present income was obviously more than adequate?

'We have a fat list of things to ask Clay about,' Lyon said.

'Uh huh,' the chief replied as he drove through the security gate leading into the project. The irate guard was obviously perplexed when the police cruiser swept past. 'Which of these miniature mansions is his?' Rocco asked.

'Follow this road to the end and turn down the cul-de-sac to the right and he's the last unit nearest the lake.'

'How can a CPA who does your taxes afford to live out here with all these yuppies?' Rocco asked as his internal police alarm clicked in.

'Like I said,' Lyon answered. 'We have a book of questions for Clay.'

They wondered if any answers were to be provided after Rocco's persistent ringing went unanswered. Clay's metallic voice finally blurted from a small unit on the wall. 'I'm too upset over my brother's death to talk with anyone today.'

Lyon nudged Rocco and pointed to Bambi's pickup parked in the drive. 'Hers,' he mouthed.

'You want I should get a warrant, Mr Dickensen?' Rocco said without a hint of warmth.

The front door jerked open as far as its chain allowed. Clay peered anxiously through the narrow opening. 'Do I need a lawyer?'

'Not if you answer a few questions.' Rocco automatically put the tip of a size-fourteen brogan into the door's aperture.

Clay looked down at the invading foot. 'I assume this is about Morgan?'

'Yep.'

'I'm really tied up right now,' Clay said. 'If you need a statement of some sort, I can meet you down at your office in an hour. OK?' He tried to shut the door without waiting for an answer.

'This will only take a few minutes,' Rocco said as he pushed the door with enough pressure to snap the chain from its mounting and slam it back against the wall. 'Oh, sorry. Don't know my own strength.'

'Hey!' Clay protested. 'You can't do that! You can't come in here unless I invite you.'

70

'Lyon has an income-tax question, and that's our reason for entry,' Rocco said.

Lyon followed Rocco inside as Clay continued protesting their entrance.

A woman's clothing trail led through the living room and out the sliding glass doors to a rear deck. The path was well marked, beginning with a blouse strewn haphazardly on the floor near the couch. A very large red bra was draped across an armchair, followed by a puddle of jeans that Lyon recognized. The path culminated with red bikini panties drooped across the metal door sill.

Clay's protest stopped abruptly as he watched them follow the clothing trail through the room and out the open doors. A nude Bambi Dolores reclined on a chaise lounge in the sun. Her head was turned to the side, with a folded towel covering her eyes.

'Our creature of the woods?' Rocco asked.

'Bambi Dolores,' Lyon answered. 'Morgan's late-night visitor.'

'Miss Dolores had a trying time,' Clay said. 'She's exhausted and really needs her rest.' He softly closed the sliding glass doors. He looked at their skeptical faces. 'She is forced to sunbathe without clothing because of her stage career. She cannot have panty and bra lines on her body that will show while she dances.'

'You just happened to run into her at Sarge's place? Over a drink, she just happened to ask if you knew a good spot for nude sunbathing?' Rocco asked as he reunited the red panties and bra.

'So, OK, I knew her from last year and we've met a few times since. One night when I was in Boston on business, Morgan called my hotel and asked me over to the Combat Zone for what he said would be a couple of laughs.' He gestured with his shoulder toward the naked woman on the deck. 'Bambi was on the runway of the White Pussy Cat doing her thing. Morgan tried to convince me that her act was a humorous and awkward example of our decadent culture, completely devoid of aesthetics. He called it a genuine piece of prurient Americana conceived and dedicated to the

71

birthplace of puritanism, Massachusetts. I saw through his scholarly observations the instant he stuffed the first twenty in her G-string.'

'Did you do any G-string stuffing?' Rocco asked.

'Bambi is a very loving and generous person,' Clay answered. 'And that sums it up. All right, fellows, you forced your way in here, so what is it that can't wait?'

'It's about Morgan,' Lyon said.

'His murder was on the TV,' Clay said. 'I assume those Satan nuts got him.'

'We see that you are overwhelmed with grief,' Rocco observed. 'And sleeping beauty on the sun deck is exhausted from her mourning.'

'It would be hypocritical for me to pretend,' Clay said. 'Lyon and others know how I felt about Morgan. As for Bambi, I have been able to make arrangements for her child, and she is most appreciative.'

'Like how appreciative for what?' Rocco asked.

'As soon as I heard about the murder, I worked out a solution with Bambi over any claims she might have against the estate.'

'Then the baby was Morgan's,' Lyon said.

'Of course. I've made arrangements with Bambi for Barney to get two hundred and fifty thousand dollars from the estate if she signs off without further legal hassles. That seems to be satisfactory with her.'

Rocco nodded. He stepped through the glass door and walked over to the nude woman. 'I'm glad she's happy with that arrangement, Clay.' He lifted the portion of the folded towel that lay over her upper face. 'Yep, real glad she's happy over that settlement, because this woman is dead.'

Eight

'What in the hell are you talking about?' Clay took three running steps toward the deck before he stopped at Rocco's raised-hand command. Rocco lifted the woman's limp wrist and let it fall. The hand fell back against her body without resistance. 'This is crazy. Ten minutes ago she was waltzing around the room peeling off her clothes in a sexy little dance.' He moved closer to the chaise lounge as Rocco stepped aside. 'Come on, Bambi, quit the . . . Oh, my God!' Clay turned away and grabbed the deck rail with both hands.

'I told you she was dead,' Rocco said, without taking his eyes from the stricken accountant. Clay nodded agreement.

Lyon found the grief-stricken man's body language very convincing. It either signified complete shock, or indicated that Clay was a consummate actor, or perhaps a complete sociopath. He knew that the amoral could don any emotional pose they desired in a manner so convincing that they could pass a lie-detector test given by the most experienced operator.

'She must have had a massive heart attack,' Clay said. He ventured another quick look at the corpse. 'Look, her body isn't disturbed and I didn't hear a sound.'

Rocco stooped by the chaise lounge and began to examine the area as much as he could without touching the body again. 'You must have heard something, Clay?' he asked.

'I swear, I didn't hear a sound. After she went out on the deck, I read the paper for a few minutes and then called my office. I told my secretary that I had to make arrangements for Morgan's funeral and wouldn't be in today. After the call, I returned to the living room and it was about then that you guys arrived . . . Don't you think we had better call nine-one-one or something?'

'You had no intention of opening the front door until we forced our way in,' Rocco pressed.

Clay shrugged toward the intimate clothing strewn around the room. 'Jesus, give me a break. It looks like we just had an orgy in here and you expected to find me in mourning.'

Rocco knelt by the body and gestured to Lyon. 'Look at the back of the head,' he said.

Lyon's combat experience may have been limited, but he had seen gunshot wounds before. In fact, he had seen more torn and mutilated bodies than he cared to remember or could ever forget.

He theorized that the narrow entrance wound near the center of Bambi's head was made by a steel-jacketed round traveling at a high muzzle velocity. The lack of powder residue or burn marks on the scalp seemed to indicate that the shot was fired from a distance. Since Clay's unit abutted the project's artificial pond, it was probable that it was fired from the other side of the lake. A small amount of blood seeped from the entrance wound. The exit wound was revealed when the towel was completely removed from her face. A mixture of bone fragments, brain matter, and congealing blood were splattered on the wall. The bullet had spent itself against the deck flooring near the glass doors.

Lyon couldn't help but reflect on this feisty woman's death. The flamboyant exotic dancer, who boasted lustily of her relationship with Morgan with a twinkle in her eye, was now devoid of all animation. Her body, the voluptuousness of which was an enticement to eroticism, had been instantly rendered into useless inert matter. Her last theatrical display would be on an autopsy table. The little boy named after a dinosaur would be raised by others. It was an unfair event that had deprived this zesty woman of over half of her life.

Rocco examined the corner where the spent bullet was embedded. 'We could dig this out, but I'll leave that up to the lab guys.'

'Which way are you going to take this?' Lyon asked.

'I've got no choice but to call in the state and let their

boy scouts run it around. We have to assume that this woman's death is tied to Morgan's. That means that the whole damn case is getting too complicated, with a hell of a lot of lab work involved. We've got to have this bullet tested, and I want some ballistics on the shot's trajectory. And that doesn't begin to include the huge crew of investigators that should be working this.'

Lyon looked across the deck toward the lake punctuated with its small island. The island was to their right, which put it out of the line of fire for Bambi's entrance wound. On the far side of the water were a cluster of condominiums under construction. The structures had been framed, but their outer walls and interiors were still unfinished. He drew an imaginary line from the partially completed buildings to the gunshot wound.

Rocco searched for the phone and found a cordless unit in a book-lined room off the hall. He called the local assistant medical examiner and the state police barracks. He returned to the dining area to straddle a straight chair and wait.

Clay came out of the lav drying his face with a small monogrammed towel.

'A woman had her head practically blown off twelve feet from where you were sitting,' Rocco said, 'and you claim you didn't hear a thing?'

'I did not hear a shot. What more can I say?'

'It was very generous of you to offer her two hundred and fifty thousand dollars knowing it would never have to be paid,' Rocco said.

'That's not the way it was, Chief.' Clay went to the kitchen, where he jerked open the refrigerator and twisted a can of diet soda off a six pack. He slumped into a chair across from Rocco and snapped the tab off the can.

'Bambi was with you the night that Morgan was killed?'

'Yes. We spent that night and last night together.'

'Did she help you kill Morgan?'

'No. After I made our deal concerning her baby, there would be no reason for her to kill Morgan.'

Rocco and Lyon exchanged quick glances. 'Interesting,'

Rocco said. 'You made your financial arrangements with Bambi before Morgan died?'

'No, of course not. But I intended to go to Morgan for it.'

'A slip of the tongue?' Lyon suggested.

'Yes, of course,' Clay said.

Rocco laced his hands behind his head and intently examined the ceiling. 'Let's look at a possible scenario. You two returned to the Wentworth house and Morgan's RV. Between one and three a.m., you talked to Morgan through the door, or maybe Bambi whispered sexy nothings through a vent. Did she give him the sex talk? Did she offer Morgan a private showing of her special dance with a finale that he could really appreciate? Or did you offer to forget the trust argument? Something was said that convinced him to drop the gate. It's my gut feeling it was her talking dirty, because Morgan wouldn't believe a word you said. Once that door opened, you forced your way in, grabbed the sword, and suddenly it was French Revolution time.'

Two police sirens could be heard in the distance.

'You know, Chief, you've really been lapping at the sauce one time too many. I think our conversation is ended until I have advice of counsel.'

A trio of state police cruisers halted in front of the condominium with a screech of tires and the despairing wail of dying sirens. Car doors slammed in alternating bursts as large troopers quickly exited and fanned around the building. A cautious pair donned wide-brimmed hats with one hand while the other gripped holstered pistol butts as they moved carefully toward the front door.

The approach of additional sirens infuriated Rocco Herbert. He rushed past the startled troopers to stand in the center of the cul-de-sac with hands on hips. Two town of Murphysville patrol cars hastily braked before they slammed into him.

'I did not call you guys!' Rocco yelled. 'Why in the hell would I want the town's entire day shift out here when I have enough smokies to begin World War Three?'

'Dispatcher caught the call on the network,' Officer Brumby said, 'and we thought . . .'

'You thought wrong. Go on now. Brumby, you got school-crossing duty in ten minutes.'

'They got to have back-up, Chief.'

More sirens approached. Another trio of state cruisers followed by a lab truck and the medical examiner's car filled the paved circle. 'Out, out, out!' Rocco bellowed at his startled patrolmen. 'I never want a double response unless the Dalton brothers are robbing the bank.'

The state police cordoned off the area and strung crime-scene tape down to the water's edge. Forensics lab personel, a photographer, and a doctor cluttered the rear deck. These were professionals who moved with a minimum of wasted motion as they efficiently unpacked equipment and made notes. When they spoke, it was in muted tones as if the reason for their presence was those who slept, not the dead.

Captain Norbert, the state police barracks commander, pulled Lyon into the kitchen while Rocco argued over jurisdictional details with an impassive state police sergeant.

'You know, Wentworth, we might give lip service to this Armageddon crap, but you're still on the shortlist of suspects. Just a warning so you don't book any overseas travel. I've got my eye on you, mister. And how come you just happen to be at the scene of another murder?'

'Ask Rocco,' Lyon said.

'I never did trust you quiet ones, because experience tells me intellectuals do the back-stabbing.' The red-faced state police captain gave Lyon another disdainful look and stalked out to the deck.

A detective trooper in plainclothes was interviewing Clay in the dining room. On the deck the photographer snapped the last of two dozen shots of the dead woman from as many different angles. Rocco flicked his finger at Lyon to signal for an outside conference.

'How did you figure the trajectory of the killing shot?' Rocco asked as they walked away from the condo.

'There's a construction site across the lake. It's the right distance, and since the wind is about twenty miles from the west, the sound wouldn't have carried. A position in one of the upper floors would give the shooter the proper elevation to account for the slight downward tilt to the wound.'

Rocco nodded. 'Sounds reasonable. Clay told me that he couldn't have driven anywhere without Bambi moving her pickup, since she had him blocked in.' They looked down the drive to see that Clay's Saab was parked directly in front of the pickup. Lyon reached inside the cab of Bambi's vehicle and popped the hood. Rocco felt the engine compartment's interior. 'She's warm,' Rocco said. 'This vehicle's been driven within the past hour.'

'Let's see if we can find out where the shot came from,' Lyon said.

Rocco casually steered the cruiser with one hand as they drove slowly out of the cul-de-sac and through the project's winding tree-lined streets. 'They raped this land bare to build these damn things, and when they finished they had to import trees. Full-grown trees which must have cost a bundle.'

They drove to the right of the lake until they reached the far side and found their way blocked by a series of tennis courts. Rocco turned the cruiser around and retraced their route. On the second attempt he drove around the left side until they came to an unpaved street that led to the units under construction.

Rocco parked by a large bundle of sheet rock and they walked along the rutted ground in front of the partially completed buildings. As he looked across the lake past the island, Lyon could easily identify Clay's condo by the flashing bubblegum lights on the police cruisers in the cul-de-sac. He could also see troopers searching the grounds around the unit where Bambi Dolores had been murdered.

Lyon stopped in front of a nearly completed unit that was in a direct line from Clay's deck. As he looked through the opening that would eventually be a doorway, he could see past the studded but unfinished rooms to the lake. A new set of uniforms had joined the state troopers at Clay's. Their faces were indistinct at this distance, but the gurney and body bag identified them.

'The geometry is right for this location,' Lyon said.

They stepped over a wooden concrete form, into what

78

would be the vestibule. The stairs hadn't been installed, but a ladder was propped conveniently in the stairwell. Rocco adjusted his revolver in its holster and slowly climbed the ladder. Near the top, he unholstered the weapon and moved cautiously ahead. He gestured down to Lyon.

'Empty. Come on up.'

The window overlooking the lake had a clear view of Clay's unit. 'This was the shooter's position,' Lyon said. 'I think when the lab guys come out here with a transit they'll be able to establish it definitely.'

Rocco bent down to reach under a two-by-four end piece near a small pile of sawdust. 'Bingo.' He held up a shell casing impaled on the end of his ballpoint pen. 'Thirty caliber.' He dropped the brass into an acetate evidence bag and walked over to the window. 'I think we had better get the lab guys to check for latent prints.'

'Do you think Clay waited until she fell asleep on the chaise lounge and then drove her truck over here? He fired from this window, probably with a telescopic sight?'

Rocco nodded agreement. 'He would have braced the rifle on the window sill. It's a clear field of fire. If he set his windage correctly, had a good rifle, and was just a moderately decent shot, he would have gotten her.'

'There are no occupied units on this side of the lake and the workmen aren't here today. There's no one on this side of the lake to hear the shot, and it was too distant, with the wind in the wrong direction, for those on the far side to hear it.'

'Yep,' Rocco said as they walked back to the cruiser. 'I think Clay and Miss Bambi did Morgan together. I believe his story about promising her the two hundred and fifty thou. That was for openers to catch her interest. A promise made before the killing. Then he got to worrying about leaving his fate in the hands of a topless dancer and decided to do away with his witness. We'll never know all that happened, but perhaps she was already pressuring him for more money, with a little sexual blackmail to sweeten the pot.'

Rocco drove in his usual nonchalant manner as he turned down the cul-de-sac filled with official vehicles. Clay burst through the front door as they parked behind the laboratory van. He ran toward Bambi's pickup. An irate Captain Norbert came out on the stoop and bellowed after him. 'Get back in here, you accounting asshole!'

Clay fumbled through his pockets until he found the proper key to turn the pickup's ignition. He ignored the angry state police officer as he drove the truck across the lawn, around the cruisers, and back to the street.

'Now we know how he started her truck,' Rocco said. He cupped his hands to yell at the irate captain. 'Hey, Norbie, your prisoner just took off!'

Norbert replied by flipping an obscene finger gesture. 'If he was under arrest, I'da shot the bastard.' He stalked back inside.

'I'm quitting this damn job,' Rocco said. 'I think I can get the nomination to run for town clerk next November and that's the way I'm going. The town clerk has regular hours and the job would put me in contact with a better bunch of people.'

'I've always felt that law enforcement was difficult because of the scum you are forced to deal with daily,' Lyon said.

'I don't mean the bad guys,' Rocco said. 'I can deal with them. I mean finks like Norbie. He's nearly as pissed now as the day I told him I was marrying Martha.'

'Why was he angry about that?' Lyon asked.

'Maybe because Martha was six months pregnant at the time. In those days, guys like Norb considered knocking up their little sister somewhere near child abuse.'

'How old was she?'

'Twenty-seven. Why do you think I'm not on the state force? He was only a sergeant then, but he was still able to poison my application.' He clicked open the driver's door and unwound to his full height. 'Let's see why Clay ran off.'

Norbie was reading the interrogation notes in the living room and glanced up at Rocco and Lyon with annoyance. 'Find anything?'

Rocco laid the acetate bag containing the shell casing on the table. 'I'll give directions to your guys to where we found it. The place should be checked for latents. The engine on the victim's pickup was still warm.'

'Your bashful bookkeeper saw you checking it out and immediately told me he borrowed it from her to get the newspaper.'

'The paper's not delivered out here?' Lyon wondered aloud.

'Why did you let our prime suspect drive off?' Rocco asked.

Norbert's complexion changed to a darker hue of red. 'Because I wanted him to grab the first flight to Brazil or Cuba or wherever in hell it is that we don't have an extradition treaty! Why in the hell do you think I let him go? He began to sweat when I laid it all out for him. He admits to owning an M-1 Garand rifle, then claims it was stolen last week. You saw the car keys he had. When I start ticking this stuff off, he finally says to me that he had best get a lawyer and off he runs.'

'You could have stopped him.'

'How? I don't have a firm case yet.'

Bea Wentworth thought she understood modern, but this place was really far out. The structure didn't resemble an ordinary house. It was a series of protruding concrete shafts that only coincidentally happened to enclose an interior where someone might live if they didn't care about normal wall space. She reversed the car back down the drive to the entrance and rechecked the address on the mailbox. It read as it had the first time: Xanadu – 71 River Road. The 71 part matched the address she had for Garth Wilkins. The Xanadu part obviously belonged to that mass of concrete planes projecting out over the hill above her. She shoved the gear into drive and went back up to the building.

She parked under the misnamed porte cochere, which really wasn't part of an entryway as much as it was a rectangular slab that seemed to accidentally extend over the drive. She searched in vain for a doorbell or knocker before realizing that a hanging gong was used for that purpose. When struck it sounded low mellow notes which were answered from the interior by a muted flute. The flute faded away as the door slid open.

81

Garth stood in the door wearing a vivid red dressing gown with leaping black dragons embroidered down the sides. The robe accentuated his slender frame. He looked at her with mild surprise. 'Why, good morning, Beatrice. What brings you to Xanadu? Not that you aren't always welcome.'

'I came to talk about Morgan. You have heard?'

'Yes, of course. It's a messy business. I only hope it doesn't require the university to expose a lot of dirty linen. I vehemently disagreed with the man on many occasions, but I wouldn't wish that death on anyone. But do come in.'

She followed him into the house aware that in this place of strange angles and linear oddity, and dressed in his bright swirling gown, Garth seemed less awkward and nearly graceful. Rooms spoked out of the entrance and consisted of long narrow spaces with gleaming hardwood floors and stark white walls. Decoration was an occasional oriental print framed in lacquered black bamboo lit by a subtle light. Entryways were either doorless or partially obscured by decorative oriental screens. There wasn't any ordinary furniture – only an occasional pillow or two placed near low tables.

'Your home is very . . . interesting,' she said. If this house was representative of his taste, Garth must consider Nutmeg Hill, with its eclectic mix of comfortable contemporary and early American pieces, a Collier brothers collection of junk.

'Thank you,' Garth responded, either ignoring or not conscious of her qualified approval. 'We are quite happy here. We were about to have brunch. Leslie has prepared his tomato surprise.'

'Oh, I really couldn't impose,' Bea said.

'Not an imposition,' Garth responded. 'But do not expect a gourmet meal with Leslie's cooking. I usually prepare most of the meals, but from time to time he insists. As the man said, do not wonder how well he does it, but that he does it at all.' He called out. 'Leslie, we have a guest. Throw on another tomato or whatever you do with those things.'

Leslie, a blond man with a wide smile that seemed to cleave his face into two parts, dried his hands on a large apron as he bustled toward them. His face brightened when he saw Bea. 'I know you!' he said exuberantly. 'You're

Senator Wentworth.' His hand shot forward to heartily grasp hers. 'You proposed the Gay Rights bill in the state legislature last session.'

'Why, yes, I did.'

'Rather unsuccessfully, I might add,' Garth said.

'It was a step,' Bea said. 'We got support from some surprising areas this time.'

'Do your thing, Les, while I show the senator around our digs,' Garth said as he steered Bea by the elbow through a tour of the house. 'We designed this place ourselves. Leslie has an architectural degree, although he's never been licensed. He seems to have difficulty in passing part three of the examination, which has to do with stresses, material strength, and other scientific facts which he detests. But if you like modern, he's actually quite good in design.'

They entered a room that seemed to serve as a sleeping area, with a wide futon and oblong windows that overlooked a Japanese garden enclosed by a waist-high wall. 'I love that garden,' Bea said with wonder.

Garth looked down with immense fondness at the narrow gravel paths, goldfish pond and a dozen different varieties of bonsai. 'I can't tell you how much the tranquility of that garden has meant to me. Sitting on that bench and absorbing its perfect dimensions saved my sanity after some of those faculty meetings. I'd come home agitated and upset and on the verge of blowing. I would sit on the bench by the bridge near the goldfish. Leslie would pour a perfect Bombay Gin and tonic and bring it to me out by the pond. It made it possible to forget Morgan for a time.'

'It would seem that your Morgan problem has been removed,' Bea said.

'That monster's not through with us yet,' Garth said bitterly. 'He's reaching from his grave to stir a cauldron of trouble in the department. There's still more misery around the corner, and Morgan knew it as he died.'

'How's that?'

'We don't have a chairman anymore, now do we? Thomas from Yale hasn't officially joined us yet, and under the circumstances, may not. Precedence at the university seems to make it clear that either Ernest or myself, as senior members of the staff, be considered for department head.' He turned to her with a wistful smile. 'So you see, he's not through with us yet.'

'The competition between you and Ernest heats up?' she asked.

'To say the least. Which means that the dirty laundry will be forced out, and that's unfortunate. Ernest will be destroyed because of the dossier that Morgan built up on him over the last two years.'

'Dossier?'

'It's nearly impossible to fire a tenured teacher unless there's a morals charge involved.'

'I've known Ernest for years,' Bea said. 'He might be sexist, but as far I know he's never done anything criminal in his life unless you include hitting on a few graduate students.'

Garth sighed. 'More than chasing grad students. It would seem that Ernest sexually harassed every female teacher or student that he managed to trap in his office for longer than five minutes. His office hours were evidently infamous to all female students and instructors. You can't get away with that sort of activity these days.'

'I'm amazed that he was so indiscreet.'

'Morgan was evidently a voyeur, but it wouldn't be hard, the way Ernest flaunts his sexuality as some sort of machismo badge.'

'Exposing Ernest places you in an odd position, Garth. If you attempt to use that type of ammunition against him, there could be repercussions.'

Garth laughed. 'My dear, the days when sexual preference could be used against me are past. I am long out of that closet, and if you will look at our home, you will see that it is a very nice open closet we inhabit.'

'Come chow down, you guys,' Leslie said from the doorway.

They moved to a dining area where a low table had been served. 'Morals charges these days, at a non-Bible-thumping school in the northeast, do not consist of sexual preferences unless you are a pedophile. In that instance, the sex of your victim is immaterial. You're thrown out.'

Bea slipped out of her shoes and sat on a cushion directly across from the two men. Leslie poured tea from a small earthen teapot and solemnly handed it to her in an exquisite porcelain cup. 'By the way, Garth,' she asked, 'the night Morgan was killed . . .'

Her incomplete question agitated Leslie to the extent that he knocked over the teapot and glared at her. 'He was here with me all night!' Leslie said quickly. 'I'll swear to that on all the stacks of holy books you have.'

'Oh, please,' Bea said as she donned her most political smile. 'I never intended to suggest . . . Surely, you don't think I was asking for an alibi while eating at your table?'

Leslie's face flushed. While Bea blushed inwardly at her lie.

Lyon Wentworth often missed teaching at Middleburg University. It was a small liberal arts school that fell into the category often referred to as 'little Ivy.' It was an old school even by northeastern standards, competitive by admission standards, expensive by financial standards, and liberal by all standards. It had one advantage over its larger and more prestigious brothers and sisters. In the powerhouse universities, the famous members of the faculty rarely taught on an undergraduate level. At Middleburg, those faculty members that enjoyed a small measure of international or national acclaim taught classes on all levels.

Lyon often missed the routine and camaraderie of academic life. This nostalgia was particularly strong on those unproductive days when he sat at his lonely computer on Nutmeg Hill and nothing happened. Eventually the Wobblies would return from wherever they'd been hiding and the feeling would pass. Still, he missed the stimulus of teaching, meeting with students, and the interaction with the faculty.

In recent years, with Morgan's tenure as chair, the department had not been filled with jolly academics. God only knows what seismic waves his death would cause.

A phone call to the department secretary told him that

Ernest had a ten o'clock class followed by office hours. Both the seminar and his office were in Blenheim.

Ernest's small book-lined office was cluttered with Hemingway memorabilia. Photographs of the author in various stages of his career and marriages covered the walls. Lyon was grateful that the size of the small office precluded exhibitions of stuffed animal heads and mounted fish. The office was adjacent to the seminar, with a connecting door ajar between them. Lyon sat on a window sill near the open door, where he could watch Ernest pace the small conference room.

The teacher was gesticulating excitedly with broad chopping motions. He had the entranced attention of five male and a single female student slouched around a circular table.

'Thud!' Ernest shouted loud enough to startle his small audience. His right fist smacked into an open palm with a loud splat. 'Ugh!' Ernest said. 'That's the way the masters write it. An eye for an eye. From the revenge of Odysseus upon the suitors to the gut-wrenching .45 shot into the belly of a naked woman in Mickey Spillane. Sword sweeps, dagger thrusts, eye-gouging, crotch kicks, and stomping to the death. Written violence,' he shouted in conclusion, 'is literature's metaphor for man's search for God!'

This seemed to signal the end of the class. Chairs squeaked, rucksacks were tossed over shoulders, and the small procession filed from the room under Ernest's benign gaze. The co-ed, dressed like her male counterparts in a loose white shirt and jeans torn at the knees, hung back behind the others. A tuft of streaked purple hair stuck straight up. Her fingers trailed lightly across Ernest's arm. 'I am enlightened,' she said. 'Thank you for sharing these insights with us, Dr Harnell.' Her hand lingered a moment longer on the teacher's arm and then she left. Lyon was convinced that she gave her bottom an extra wiggle as she preened under Ernest's appreciative lechery.

'You seem to have a true admirer, Doctor,' Lyon said from his seat on the window sill.

Ernest shrugged. 'That comes from her complete immersion

into the material of the course. She's a very sensitive young woman. We can't call them girls anymore, you know.'

'So I've heard,' Lyon said, and wondered how much immersion Ernest had in that particular student.

'That's an interesting class you were teaching,' Lyon said as Ernest came into the office and leafed through a short list of phone messages. 'Something new, I gather?'

'Yes, it's been moderately popular,' the teacher said. 'They made me tone down the course description for the catalog, but the truly interested students pick up on it through the underground grapevine. The high point of the syllabus was last week's discussion: "The Marquis de Sade as the antecedent of non-violence."' He held up a message slip. 'Here's one. It's a fax from Thomas at Yale turning down the Ashley chair. The wimp didn't even have enough courtesy to talk to one of us in person. I guess that conveniently rules him out. I think, Mr Wentworth, that you just might be looking at the next chairman of the English department of Middleburg University.'

'Wouldn't it be slightly premature to offer congratulations before the official vote, Ernest?'

'It's practically a foregone conclusion. The competition was only between me and Garth, and they certainly can't give it to him, because of the morals question.'

'Do you mean they'll rule him out because of homosexuality?'

'Hell, no! I'm talking pedophilia here. Morgan had the complete gen on the man. He had documented evidence that Garth was having sexual relations with underage male students, and that is a hanging offense. That skinny fag is a long drink of water drawn from a poisoned well. If we had him on safari in Africa he'd be shot in the bush.'

'What's happened to this documentation now that Morgan's dead?'

'It's in his office. I know the locked file where he kept his budget recommendations and personnel files, and whatever else his viper brain wanted to hoard.'

'Isn't his office on this floor?'

'Down the hall.'

'Can we get in?'

'Yes,' Ernest nodded.

'I'm surprised the police haven't sealed it off.'

'They called and said they were obtaining a warrant.'

'Then we had better get inside before someone else does.'

Ernest blanched. 'I hadn't considered that someone might get in those files. Jesus, if anything happened to that dirt on Garth . . .'

'Let's check it out,' Lyon said. They hurried down the hall toward the front of the building and Morgan's corner office.

As soon as Ernest opened the office door with a master key, it was apparent that the office had been ransacked. The drawers of three file cabinets along the far wall were pulled out and their contents strewn across the floor. The desk had been crudely forced open, and the drawers were pulled from the frame and overturned. Their contents left a messy paper trail across the room.

'I'll be damned!' Ernest said. 'Look.' He pointed to a spot on the wall behind the desk, where the unmistakable outline of a sword marred the wall.

'Where was the locked cabinet with the personal files?' Lyon asked.

'Behind his desk. The one with the front pried open.'

The dented front and sides clearly indicated that a sharp instrument, perhaps a chisel, had been inserted with enough force to pop the sheet metal away from the frame. The box was completely empty.

'Someone took the entire contents of the top drawer,' Lyon said as he turned to face Ernest.

'That was the one with the important stuff in it.'

'And yet the office outer door wasn't forced. Who has a key to this place?' Lyon asked.

'Jesus, Lyon, half the town of Middleburg. Garth for openers, and the department secretary. Then there's maintenance, and of course security. I suppose a couple of the deans would have access. Who knows?'

'Where were you when Morgan was killed?' Lyon asked.

'Home,' Ernest whispered. 'After I left your place, I went

directly home . . . alone . . . My sister was already asleep. For the rest of the night no one saw me until I came to work the next morning.'

Nine

Bea Wentworth despised shopping malls in direct proportion to their size and the amount of time she was required to spend in them. Occasionally this feeling created a faint twinge of jingoistic guilt as it seemed slightly un-American, a trifle antisocial, and a bit inconvenient. She had finally forced herself to accept these suburban behemoths peopled with bored teenage clerks and recognize that they had irrevocably replaced individually owned local stores staffed by owners who knew their products.

Her worst mall fear was interception by predatory constituents. Voters who tracked you were usually motivated to a feeding frenzy by some obsessive cause. They were able to detect the faintest of legislative spoors as they pursued their prey.

Her mall attackers were usually white males of the Korean War generation. They were often life members of the American Legion with a vaguely assigned responsibility to run her to ground. Contrary to any provisions of the United States Constitution, recent supreme court rulings, or common decency, this breed of constituent demanded immediate legislation concerning school prayer (put back), sex education programs (take out), or welfare cheats (kill soon).

As a consequence, during her absolutely necessary shopping forays, she wore dark glasses and a floppy hat that obscured most of her face. Her movements consisted of furtive darts from store to store, similar to the avoidance trail made by a small scurrying rodent.

New garden gloves and a small trowel led today's shopping list. Sears was the store of choice for those items, but she must be careful to make a wide circle around the power tools section, which was a popular holding area for the American Legion contingent.

It was going to be intriguing to watch the look on Senator Beatrice Wentworth's face as she died. A silent method would best serve the day. Such close work would require a minor disguise. Broad sunglasses, nondescript clothing, and a hat tilted over the face should be adequate. Recognition might come in her last seconds, but then it would be too late.

The handle of the rolled umbrella separated to reveal a long stiletto-like knife blade. The fatal blow would be a quick thrust to the left of the sternum with the knife pointed to the shoulder. Once the blade had fully penetrated, it would be rotated until the steel ripped the ventricular muscle of the heart. Blood would be rapidly pumped into the thoracic cavity rather than the aorta. She would be conscious long enough to see the blade enter, realize the implication of the act and then fall into an agonizing unconsciousness so quickly she would only utter a single sound of protest. The knife would be reinserted into the umbrella.

The complete murder sequence would take seconds. Wentworth would die curled on some shop floor under a counter of women's handbags. The body would quickly be surrounded by a mix of the curious, morbidly interested, and the horrified. The majority of the onlookers would be acne-infected teenagers whose reaction to the death would be a slight increase in their gum-chewing rate. The knife would have been withdrawn and reinserted into the umbrella. The gathering crowd would make an excellent escape screen.

Yes, that was the way it would be. A quick knife thrust followed by a virtual disappearance. Now, the only detail remaining was to find the opportune place. It was fitting that this interfering woman's death would be by a different method than the others. Her murder while in the center of a crowd would be appropriate.

Bea found new meaning in the term 'horns of a dilemma'. When the store's elevator door swished shut behind her, she saw Ralston Proman directly ahead. Ralston was a professional Korean War Veteran whose mission in life was the creation of a state memorial to his war.

His spiel was a repetitious ten-minute harangue. This speech always seemed to segue into sexual innuendoes culminating with an invitation to the legion post bar for a couple of quick pops.

The only avenue of escape was down a side aisle where Martha Herbert was browsing at a perfume counter. Martha's concentration on an examination of a small bottle of Red might allow Bea to slip by behind her. Martha, for unknown reasons, had been cool lately, but a possible slight by her was preferable to an overwhelming onslaught by former PFC Ralston Proman. Making a decision, she began a skulking slither past the perfume counter.

She had nearly slipped past when Martha decided to sample. She held a small vial of Red in her hand as she peered into the counter mirror to spray a daub behind her ear. Bea's reflection startled her and her reflexive turn made the perfume atomizer point at Bea like a threatening can of mace.

Bea held up her hands. 'Hi, don't shoot.'

Martha squinted in surprise and broke eye contact to look past Bea at the person behind them in the aisle. Bea stepped aside as the umbrella bearer swept past the counter and continued through the store.

'Have time for coffee?' Bea asked.

'There's a gourmet coffee shop down the way a bit,' Martha said softly.

They sat at a small marble table with demitasse cups of Swiss chocolate almond coffee. 'Since this mall opened it's revolutionized my shopping life and destroyed our budget,' Martha said in a valiant attempt to steer their meeting to a light area.

Bea knew that a recapitulation of her feelings about shopping malls and their destruction of downtown centers would appear to be an affront to Martha. 'Filene's seems to have some good sales,' she finally dredged from some remote part of her mind.

*   *   *

It was possible to see into the coffee shop from the heavy wooden bench against the rail in the mall's upper walkway. The oblique line of sight meant that the observer was unseen.

The two women inside the shop appeared to be talking intimately over their coffee. That reoriented the situation and required a slightly different mode of attack. The original assumption had Bea Wentworth alone in a crowd. It was assumed that she would not be known by anyone in the immediate murder area. This chance meeting with a friend altered that.

It would be impossible to kill both women simultaneously with the umbrella blade. A delay of even seconds between the first and second knife thrust created a dangerous situation. That interval was long enough for a potential reaction. There could be time for a scuffle, or a scream that might alert security guards and focus the attention of a crowd.

Another form of attack must be planned. That woman could not be allowed to live.

Martha looked over the rim of her cup. 'I hope everything is working out about that Morgan mess and Lyon.'

'I'm sure it will,' Bea answered. 'One thing that bothers me is that crazy idea your brother has concerning my relationship with Morgan.'

Martha seemed to give a start. 'Probably just some unfounded gossip.'

'Yes, something like that.' Pieces began to fall into place. 'I don't suppose the talk could have possibly started with someone you know?'

'Does it really matter now that he's dead?'

'It matters a great deal to me. I'd like to find out where it started,' Bea answered. 'And why.'

The umbrella weapon had been replaced by two thin knives. They nestled in special easy-draw sheaths sewn into deep side pockets of the khaki raincoat. The two women in the coffee shop were still deep in conversation and seemed to have hardly moved since the round-trip to the parking lot to obtain the knives.

It would be a simultaneous double killing. Neither woman would have an opportunity to cry out. The attack would begin when they left the coffee shop and turned into the atrium's walk. They would walk abreast. Both knives would be drawn together in a single fluid movement and plunged between their breasts at the same time.

They would fall like spent rag dolls and tumble over each other in an intertwined heap of corpses. The incongruity of their appearance would attract instant horrified attention and make it a simple matter to walk the eight steps to the escalator and descend to the main floor. Mingling with the crowd in front of Burger King would be the necessary cloak before walking briskly to the parking lot and the waiting van.

There was a certain satisfaction in committing a murder in front of a dozen witnesses and getting away with it. Bystanders were notoriously confused in their eyewitness identifications. It would be quite amusing to watch tonight's television news of the slaying.

Wait patiently. They would soon finish their coffees and step into the atrium to meet their fate.

'I can't help you,' Martha said after a pause. 'There's nothing I can say. If I knew of anything between you and someone else, or heard a rumor, I would certainly tell you.'

Bea wasn't altogether sure that she believed Martha. She had known this woman for years, although they had never been close friends. There was something about the stiffness of her response, and her pronounced shift of attention, that signified an uncomfortable attitude. 'I'm sorry you don't feel free enough to share the information with me,' Bea said.

'I said I really don't know anything, Beatrice.' This time the response was rapid and immediate. 'I know you don't respect me very much, because I stayed home and took care of my child all these years while you went into the world and did politics and important things. I'm old-fashioned and that's the way I'm made. And I am sorry you feel I'm a nothing. I am even sorrier that my husband thinks you're some sort of goddess.' Without a further word, Martha gathered her pocketbook and stiffly left the restaurant.

Bea was stunned as she looked after the departing woman. Didn't Martha remember that the child Bea would have looked after was killed in a bicycle accident ten long years ago?

She paid the check and walked to the door to discover that the day was sliding downhill at a faster velocity than she had imagined. Ralston Proman, professional legionnaire and Korean War Veteran, slouched on a bench in the walkway. He sat next to a newspaper reader wearing a voluminous khaki raincoat. Even Ralston's aging soldier eyes would spot her the moment she left the shop. Her capture would invariably lead to elbow grabbing and the commencement of the memorial harangue.

She knew from past experience in constituent escapes that there was an employee's exit to the parking lot through the back room of the coffee shop. She hoped the staff wouldn't mind her slipping out that way again.

Lyon sat before his computer monitor and stared at the blank screen that was inhabited only by an impatiently blinking cursor. That damn flickering little light made him miss his ancient Underwood Number Five typewriter. That Underwood was a real writing machine. When you pounded keys into a pockety rhythm and slapped the return after the bell pinged, you knew you were really at work, and so did anyone else within a fifty-yard radius. The silent computer stared back with its brooding blink of light that served as a reproach for words not written.

Morgan and Bambi, the incongruous dead lovers, seemed to stand on either side of the machine as quiet sentinels that forbad any creative work. His Wobbly creations would sleep until the dead were properly laid to rest.

Lyon couldn't see Nutmeg Hill's long drive from the study window, but he heard a car spewing gravel as it braked to a stop near the front door. Only one person drove up the winding drive at that rate of speed. He knew that Rocco Herbert would shortly appear in the study doorway.

It took several minutes before his grumpy friend arrived. Rocco slumped into the large leather chair. 'I'm out here on another complaint. The project manager from the condo next door called again. More graffiti has been discovered, old top.'

'Like what words of wisdom this time?'

'How about, "Beyond here there be monsters", spray painted in letters four feet tall along one wall.'

'I like the ring to that.'

'They know it's you. I know it's you, and we're both going to get our ass in a sling if you don't stop it.'

'A couple of questions about the Morgan case. Were there any prints on the shell casing we found? Secondly, were they able to lift any prints from the shooter's firing position in the unfinished unit across the lake from Clay's place?'

'Negative on both counts.'

'Also, who delivered the note the Brotherhood of Beelzebub sent to you? The one where they assumed responsibility for Morgan's killing.'

'The dispatcher thinks it was a kid who slid the envelope through the reception window. She was on a unit dispatch at the time, but she vaguely recalls thinking that it was the paper boy handing in his bill. Based on that, we assume it was a boy under high-school age. Because of his size, we suspect he's in the middle school. I got the word out to Joe Shattick, the principal over there, and he's talking to the teachers. So, we'll see what they turn up.'

'Have you been in contact with university security as to who might have ransacked Morgan's office?'

'Affirmative and there's nothing hard there either. Half the university had a key to that room and a four-year-old could have broken into it with an expired credit card. Since some incriminating files on Ernest and Garth are both missing, we can make an assumption that narrows it down a bit.'

'I thought Morgan's dossier was on Garth?'

'It depends on who you talk to.' Rocco flipped a small pad out of his breast pocket and flipped through half a dozen pages. 'The faculty seems to break into two distinct camps on this question. One group says Ernest tried to make it with every adult female within a five-mile radius and was now lowering his age requirements. When I start talking pedophilia, a second group points out to me that the word does not denote gender, only children. Some of this contingent leans toward Garth lusting after younger boys now that he's aging, but no one seems to have any firm knowledge either way. It's very difficult interviewing a bunch of academics, Lyon. Those who say they are the politically correct group vote for Ernest as villain. Near as I can figure, female sexual harassment is *the* crime this year. Like I said, it's very tiring work.'

'What about Clay's situation?'

'Norbie is still in touch with the state's attorney over that. I don't know if they're going for a murder warrant or not, but for the moment he's definitely their numero uno suspect, along with unknown terrorists, followed by a certain children's book writer.'

It would be a long shot of nearly four hundred yards, but the shooter had made difficult hits like that before. The one that took out Miss Big Boobs, the exotic dancer, was only slightly less than that distance, and that target was far smaller. The top of a woman's head at 400 meters is one hell of a small target area.

Bea Wentworth was clearly outlined against the stone facade of the house's parapet as she worked in her garden. She wore shorts, a loose peasant blouse scooped deep at the neck, and that same floppy hat that cast part of her face in shadows. Occasionally she stooped or kneeled to work things into the soil. When she stood, she unconsciously brushed clods of dirt from her knees.

The best time to make the shot would be when she was in a kneeling position. At that time she would be without any forward momentum and nearly motionless. She would be in a direct line in front of the rifle and clearly outlined in the sight. The trees were motionless, and the clouds hung in the sky as if suspended there by the gods. There would be no necessity to adjust for wind on this perfectly still day. The light was still good and would remain so for at least half an hour.

The mall hit would have been entertainingly different, but that opportunity was past. It was often best to rely on the old standards, for in the long run they were the most reliable.

The marksman assumed a prone position between a small boulder and a large pine. The rifle rested on a low stump, with the sling intertwined along the arm for further support.

Take time. Take careful aim. One carefully placed shot in a vital area. Easy. Breathe in and out with slow regularity and then carefully squeeze it off.

Bea Wentworth walked along the rear of the house thinking about Garth's Japanese garden with its intricate planning and tiny but perfectly formed bonsai trees. All of his shrubs, walks and ponds were sculptured into an artificial nature.

They made her plantings seem careless and haphazard. It was like comparing oriental art to a Grandma Moses primitive.

Still, she loved her mountain laurel, which bloomed early, with lovely flowers that hung from its top branches like miniature clouds. The primrose was also out. Tiers of rosettes of large lime-green leaves and small flowers surrounding the stem had a natural uninhibited beauty that she adored.

The other flowers would bloom in progression. She hoped that this year she finally had gotten it phased so that the blooming would continue through the spring, into the summer and deep into fall and Indian summer.

There was something about her visit to Garth's home that bothered her. She accepted his decor and garden, and although they were not to her own taste, she found them immensely interesting and attractive. Something had been said or done that did not quite fit. The exact nature of what she was reaching for eluded her.

She was startled by the roar of the patrol car's engine as it rocked down the drive and swerved on to the secondary highway that passed below their home. She shook her head as Lyon came out on the patio and looked down at her.

'Someone ought to give that man a ticket,' she said. 'He's become a menace on the highways.'

'He's in a hurry to get to an important appointment at Sarge's place,' Lyon said as he descended the patio steps and walked over to the garden.

'I've been thinking about my luncheon with Garth and Leslie. Something there bothers me. I think it's Leslie's reaction when I asked about the night of the murder.'

'He responded too quickly.'

'Exactly,' Bea said. 'Without thought, reflection or consideration. It was a protective reaction.'

Lyon laughed. 'That's about the feeling I had when Ernest and I discovered the mess in Morgan's office. He didn't seem nearly as surprised as I would have expected. Which is rather unusual, since the material in the file was supposed to be dirty linen that would hang Garth.'

'If Ernest suspected that Morgan had a file on him, as Garth believes, he might have gone after it. He would have to steal both files in order to not be implicated in the theft.'

'And Ernest has no alibi for the night of Morgan's murder,' Lyon said.

'Which puts us back on square one,' Bea said.

The sniper realized that now there was an opportunity to get both of them. A full clip had been inserted into the rifle's magazine and a live round levered into the chamber. After the first shot, if the remaining Wentworth didn't immediately hit the dirt, there would be a chance for a second round to take him out. It would work. Two for the price of one – delicious. The only question remaining was, which one to take first?

It was a question that required careful consideration. There was also the possibility of letting him survive a few seconds to feel the anguish of seeing her die before his eyes. A lovely choice that required a moment's deliberation.

'I ran into Martha Herbert today. I think my Morgan rumor started with her, and that bothers me.'

'I always thought you liked the strong silent type, which pretty much precluded Morgan.'

'Maybe I never told you my secret lusts,' she said as she looked down the river toward the distant Sound. She felt his arm go over her shoulder as he slowly turned her to face him.

'It's warm out here even at sunset,' Lyon said. 'Is that why you're wearing that blouse?'

'I like working in my garden unencumbered,' she said as she pulled the blouse far off her shoulders. She flicked the brim of the floppy hat to tip it off her head.

'At least we won't have to dress for dinner,' Lyon said as he kissed her.

What in the hell were they doing?

That little sexy action meant that she was going to go first. The round would be placed directly in the middle of her forehead while she stood flaunting her body. Her limbs would splay out as her head exploded over him. He would watch in horror while the second round caught her in the guts or the middle of the back. The second round wouldn't be really necessary, but the shock to him was worth the effort.

What in the hell were they doing down there?

'Don't do that!' the sniper said aloud for no one to hear. 'Are you two nuts?'

There was no possible field of fire while they were locked together on the ground between the flower beds.

How had they known? What inner sense had whispered to them that death was imminent?

Oh, my God. They were barely visible behind the mound as more clothing cluttered the primrose. Damn them! In minutes the light would be gone and the shot would be impossible.

The fools were making love while it was time to die.

Ten

'The mountain laurel is ringing,' Lyon whispered into the ear nestled against his shoulder.

'Uh huh. Don't answer,' Bea mumbled.

'It's a very persistent laurel,' he replied as the ringing continued.

She didn't answer but spooned herself closer to him for warmth.

He wrapped his arms around her to let his body heat warm her. She stopped shivering and slipped back into sleep. Her comfort had been accomplished through a heat transfer and now it was his turn to be chilled. The cold shocked him fully awake. It was dark. They'd fallen asleep between the flower beds and now the phone was ringing in the mountain laurel. He separated from her and crawled into the garden. A pebble dug into his knee and he muttered an involuntary gasp of pain.

He found it. His fingers curled around the cordless phone she always brought into the garden while she worked. He rolled over to watch the stars and clicked the talk button. 'I hope this is an extremely significant message,' he said in the most sonorous voice he could muster. 'If you are conducting a poll or selling anything, prepare for an immediate disconnect.'

'This is Leslie. I'm Garth's friend,' an alarmed voice said. 'I must speak with Mrs Wentworth immediately.'

'I'm here,' Bea said at Lyon's ear as she took the phone. 'Yes, Leslie?' She replied in a coherent voice that belied her sleepy responses of a few moments ago.

'Can you help us, Mrs Wentworth? Garth has just stormed out of the house carrying the .45 pistol that he brought back from the army.'

'Where's he going?'

'The last thing he said to me was, "I'm going to blow that Hemingway poseur to hell." I took that to mean that he intends to shoot Ernest Harnell – several times.'

'Tell me exactly what happened, Leslie.'

'Less than half an hour ago the dean of students telephoned. Garth said that it began as a perfectly ordinary conversation, but it soon became obvious that the dean was fishing for information. As the conversation continued, the dean's remarks shifted toward behavioral standards for the new department head. Then the comments began to get more pointed and personal. Garth finally asked where it was all leading and was told that an anonymous source had accused him of pedophilia.'

Bea covered the phone's mouthpiece and mouthed, 'Oh, my God.' When she resumed the conversation, she forced her voice into an optimistic lilt. 'The accusation may not be as serious as you think, Leslie. The school is not going to take any action based on undocumented accusations. The days of witch hunts are over.' She covered the mouthpiece again. 'Maybe,' she mumbled to Lyon.

'Those of us in the gay community know that the gay bashers are still active.'

'If the dean didn't identify the accuser, why does Garth want to kill Ernest?'

'Who else could it be? I watched him load the gun and saw the look on his face. There's not the slightest doubt that he's serious about this,' Leslie said. 'I thought you seemed sympathetic, and since you and your husband know them both and are connected to the university, perhaps something discreet could be done.'

'We'll do what we can,' Bea said. She ended the conversation and impatiently punched in a phone number. The police dispatcher told her that Rocco was out on a prolonged domestic-violence call, but that Jamie Martin was available. Bea rang off. 'Rocco's off on a call. We don't want Jamie on this, do we?' she asked Lyon.

'I think not.'

'Then what? If we call the state police, Norbie will probably unleash a SWAT team.'

'We get dressed and do it,' Lyon said as they hurried into the house.

Ernest Harnell lived in an eighteenth-century merchant's house that squatted directly at the sidewalk on the edge of the Murphysville town green. Similar to a dozen other homes in the neighborhood, on the corner of the second story was a historical plaque designating the original owner and date of construction. The gleaming white facade with black trim was broken by long leaded windows and a wide front door dominated by a large brass knocker. Lyon raised the lion-head hammer and let it fall three times in rapid succession.

The door was opened by a short woman with a no-nonsense scowl designed to discourage casual callers. She squinted at them a moment until recognition dredged up a wispy smile. 'Why, hello, Beatrice. So nice to see you. Do come in.' She swooped open the door and beckoned them inside.

'Your home is beautiful as always,' Bea said to Ernest's sister as she glanced into the immaculate front parlor filled with museum-quality early American antiques. 'Are you going to open the house for the Garden Club tour this year?'

'Oh, yes. I always do, no matter how much Ernest objects. I don't pay a bit of attention to his carrying on. When it's house-tour time, I make him go down to Key West to play Hemingway for a week.'

'Can we see him right away?' Lyon said. 'It's rather important.'

The diminutive woman sighed. 'Everything is always urgent when it comes to Ernest. He's in the extension cleaning his guns again.' They followed her down the wide main hall that bisected the original structure. It turned into a narrow corridor when it entered the new wing at the rear of the building. The door to a large sitting room was open. Heavy leather furnishings were surrounded by gun cabinets and mounted animal heads. The decor was of a Teddy Roosevelt rather than early New England era.

Ernest sat Indian fashion on a wide leather ottoman in front of the largest cabinet. He was carefully polishing the intricately carved stock of a large-caliber rifle with a soft cloth. He looked up as they entered, worked the bolt and thumbed off the safety. He aimed the rifle at Lyon.

'Elephant gun,' he said as he squeezed the trigger. The firing pin clicked against an empty chamber. 'This baby will bring down the biggest they grow.'

'Don't you ever point a rifle at me again,' Lyon said in a voice tinged with anger. The last time Bea recalled that tone was the night he lectured the zoning commission after their approval of the neighboring condominium.

'Hell and damnation, Mr W, it's not loaded.'

'All weapons are always loaded,' Lyon snapped.

'We'd like you to check into a hotel in Hartford for several days,' Bea said.

Ernest smirked. 'That's a terrific idea, Bea.'

'Don't be snide,' Bea said. 'Garth is on his way over here to kill you. I believe you know the reason why.'

Ernest laughed. 'I am truly frightened. I'm sitting here with an elephant gun on my lap. There's probably a thousand rounds of ammunition within arm's reach, and I'm supposed to cower because Garthy Poo is on his way over to slap me with a wet noodle?'

'Actually, the weapon of the day is a .45 caliber automatic,' Lyon said.

'I know, the only handgun he owns. It hasn't been fired in twenty years and the ammunition is probably rusted in the barrel.' He slapped the stock of the rifle on his lap. 'Not like my baby here. This sucker is loaded for bear and primed for elephants.'

'You can't hunt those anymore, Ernest,' Lyon said. 'There's an embargo on ivory. In Kenya they shoot people they find poaching.'

Ernest went to the room's largest gun cabinet next to a bookcase filled with a collection of Hemingway first editions. He opened a long drawer at its base that was filled with cartons of ammunition. He grabbed a handful of shells and crammed several into the rifle's magazine. 'I have African friends who can get around those technicalities.'

'You mount another trophy in here and I am going to be ill,' Bea said.

'Man is a predatory beast destined to hunt wild creatures,' Ernest said. 'God, I miss the green hills of Africa.'

'You're going to miss the rest of your life if you don't leave until Garth calms down,' Lyon said.

'Garth has no intention of calming down,' a voice said from the doorway. Garth slowly entered the room with a large automatic extended in front of him. He activated the slide to chamber a round with a clack that sounded louder than it actually was. He pointed the handgun directly at Ernest's forehead. 'It's death in the afternoon, Bwana.'

Ernest faced his adversary with the rifle at his waist and his finger on the trigger. 'I'm loaded for big game, Tinkerbell.'

'You sniveling son-of-a-bitch!' Garth snapped. 'Why in the hell did you tell the dean that I was involved with children!'

'I happen to know that you were arrested in Mississippi on a sex offense,' Ernest said.

'How the hell did you know that? Morgan was the only person in this state who had that information.'

'I have my sources.'

'All right, so I was. They charged me with lewd behavior, but it should have been stupidity. I was in a bar in Biloxi, Mississippi, which was mistake one. I made a date with a crew-cut guy, which was stupid mistake two. He turned out to be a deputy. At least he was thirty-eight years old, for Christ's sake! What I did wasn't nearly as criminal as your deal with what's her name? Darlene, wasn't it?'

'That girl had a woman's full equipment,' Ernest said proudly.

'Except that it was sixteen-year-old equipment. Morgan had one hell of a time getting you out of that one.'

'It was a natural mistake. I picked her up in a dimly lit bar where she wasn't legally supposed to be.'

'You should have known she was underage by the Barbie doll she was carrying.'

'She lied to me.'

In an unspoken agreement, Lyon moved clockwise and Bea counterclockwise around the perimeter of the room. They had selected their objectives without words. Lyon would disarm Ernest while Bea went for Garth's pistol. The two antagonists seemed unaware of the Wentworths' movement.

'You two are being very childish,' Bea said.

'Stay out of the line of fire,' Ernest replied. 'Tinkerbell is going to Never Never Land.'

'Good God, Ernest! Can't you be more original than that?' Garth snorted.

'I'll polish my eulogy for you.'

When they were in position a few feet on either side of the two men with the weapons, Lyon nodded at Bea, who acknowledged the signal.

They stepped toward their targets. Bea grabbed Garth's wrist with both hands and pushed his arm toward the ceiling. Lyon deflected the stock of Ernest's rifle toward the floor as he wrenched it from the other man's grasp.

Lyon slung the rifle over his shoulder and went to help Bea take the pistol from Garth. It occurred to him that possibly they had allowed themselves to be disarmed as a solution to the impasse.

'I am astonished at you two,' Bea said. 'Is that pistol registered, Garth?'

'It's a war souvenir.'

'It still has to be licensed. Both of you are guilty of assault, but of course you know that. You are also guilty of weapons charges. If you were arrested on either charge it would end the question of who chairs what very quickly.'

'You both knew about the charges against each other,' Lyon said. 'How come? Which one of you has Morgan's stolen file?'

They shook their heads in denial.

'Morgan was at Xanadu for dinner around the first of the year,' Garth said. 'He began to laugh about Ernest's claim to be the great white hunter, since his eyesight was so bad. He chortled and said a man who couldn't spot an underage girl was going to have difficulty in the bush. That's when he told us about the Darlene incident.'

Ernest looked stunned. 'My sister and I had him over for dinner last winter. When he started to talk about the Biloxi incident, I thought it was too much wine . . .'

106

'Too much sadism,' Bea said. 'It all sounds pretty calculated to me.'

'If he wasn't already dead . . .' Garth started to say.

'We could do it together,' Ernest finished.

Lyon and Bea looked at each other with a glance that wondered if perhaps there was more truth to Ernest's facetious remark than intended. It might be possible that these arch enemies were far more cooperative than previously believed.

Rina Dickensen's Exercise Place was an isolated brick building located on Route 154 near its intersection with Hilltop Road. Lyon pulled into the wide parking lot and parked behind Rina's van. He sipped the last of lukewarm coffee in its Styrofoam container. It was nearly ten a.m. and the health club's answering service had told him that Rina would have free time after her nine o'clock class.

Rina and Skee had refurbished the building, which had a varied history before their occupancy. It had originally been a movie theater with an adjacent ice-cream parlor. For two decades it had been a popular dating place for the young, but had closed after the mall opened a multiplex cinema with six movie screens. A dinner theater replaced the movie theatre. Poor talent and worse food quickly forced bankruptcy. The next owners, who seemed to have murky Providence mob connections, opened a topless nightclub with overly ambitious barmaids. It took Rocco's constant patrols and Bea's intervention with the state liquor commission nearly nine months to hound them out of existence. The building had been vacant for nearly two years until leased by Rina and remodeled into her Exercise Place, with an adjoining health-food store.

Lyon wondered if there was a parable of our times in the building's history.

The Exercise Place layout channeled customers through the health food in order to reach the workout rooms and gym area in the rear.

Lyon walked down an aisle surrounded by shelves of beta carotene and antioxidants. Massive exercise equipment loomed at the rear of the store. Every item seemed to critique his sedentary lifestyle. Their diet at Nutmeg Hill had a high protein concentration, with liberal servings of breads, pastas and sauces. His work at the computer screen kept him nearly motionless for hours. This combination probably foretold massive health problems lurking around some distant corner. *Well, at least I don't smoke*, he thought.

Music overwhelmed him the instant he pushed through the double doors into the club's reception area. Speakers mounted on either side of the observation window that over-looked the aerobic exercise area blared a loud rendition of Tchaikovsky's 1812 Overture. The crescendo accompanied by cannon fire meant that Moscow had been captured, but the Russians were counterattacking. He stood at the window watching a dozen bodies attempting to sync with the rather bizarre exercise music. Rina, in a tight black leotard, led the exercises from a low platform.

The women's violent thrashing increased as the music swelled to a climax. Clenched hands and strained faces indi-cated maximum exertion. Rina's face was impassive as she reached out to exhort the others to increased effort. The pace of their movements increased as the music reached its final notes.

Many of the participants sank to the floor in exhaustion when the music faded, while others bent over to grasp their knees and gasp for breath. Rina left the platform and imme-diately went through a door at the rear.

The women slowly recovered and began to file silently through the reception area toward the dressing rooms. Some glared at him with suspicion, while others seemed disinter-ested to the point of disorientation.

On the far side of the workout room was a hallway which led to the rear area that had swallowed Rina. He walked down the hall to a door marked *office*. He heard a shower running as he knocked.

'Come in, Lyon,' she called through closed doors. 'It's open.'

He stepped into a combination living-office space. In one corner a simple table with graceful lines and fluted legs acted as a desk. A computer and fax machine were nearby. A living-room section composed of a couch and easy chairs grouped around a lobster-pot coffee table occupied the center of the room. The far corner contained a kitchen partitioned by a bar counter flanked with tall-backed stools. The walls contained photographs, awards and mixed memorabilia in an eclectic mixture of sporting events, rock groups, and photographs of soaring eagles.

'How did you know it was me?' he called over the running shower.

'Saw you watching the session,' she said as the door to the shower room swung back against the wall. Rina stepped out of the shower on to a thick shag rug and reached for a large terry-cloth towel.

Lyon was not surprised at the sight of her body, but he was disturbed at the extent of his own arousal. He would have thought that after last night's session in the mountain laurel that his urges would be under better control. There was a fascinating attraction in her lithe body movements. She dried herself in slow circular sweeps that were so lingering as to be erotic. He was astonished at the animal sensuality she exuded.

She turned to face him with a feral look of seduction that somehow combined with animal innocence. He felt that he was in a situation where he must either respond to her seduction or ignore it with an act of complacent normality.

'Your students didn't seem to be having much fun,' he said after opting for normalcy.

'They're not supposed to enjoy. My classes aren't designed to tuck in tummies and make them more agile bed partners. My method teaches political awareness and emphasizes feminine power.'

'I never thought of Napoleon's invasion of Russia as a women's cause.'

She stiffened. The towel fluttered forgotten to the floor. 'As a man, you'd prefer Ravel's Bolero? Or possibly a brassy striptease theme? Overture has testosterone! Got that, Wentworth? My women get power hormones!'

'An interesting concept,' Lyon agreed. He wondered why

his present life seemed so involved with a man fascinated with cojones and a female sexual acrobat intrigued with male hormones. 'Actually, I'm married to an active feminist,' he said casually as a bridge to end this avenue of conversation.

'You don't really think that? You don't really think Bea is a feminist? How can you possibly believe that she helps the cause?'

'Her political record speaks for itself.'

'It certainly does!' Her anger was so apparent that Lyon had the momentary feeling he had released some mythological beast. 'In the black community an Uncle Tom is despicable. Among the sisterhood, your wife, the infamous Senator Wentworth, is an Aunt Beatrice. She is a sycophant who throws sops to women by introducing a few inconsequential bills dictated by the male-dominated power elite.'

'Wait a minute, Rina. Her work on maternity leave and child-care centers has gotten national attention.'

'Of course!' The phrase was delivered in a shout. 'Because she is doing their bidding! We are oppressed! We do not need to have our real needs hidden by such subterfuge. She gives us a few minor laws while our bodies scream for real nourishment.'

'Why am I defending my wife's politics to a naked lady?' Lyon said aloud in a wondering tone.

'Because for once you are confronted with a real woman. An Aunt Beatrice wears cute little nighties to bed. An Aunt Beatrice lies coyly on the pillows making a childlike smile as she attempts to entice a man.'

'Recently she's been interested in flower beds, but that's something I'm not getting into. Rina, I am not going to argue my wife with you. Now, where's Skee?'

The tension immediately left her body as if she had suddenly become completely disinterested in the argument. Her enigmatic smile returned. 'I give the aerobic classes and Skee handles the gym. We'll find him there as soon as we finish.' She walked toward him with a pronounced sway of her hips. She placed the towel in his hands and turned. 'Do my back.'

Lyon fought the temptation. 'I only do one woman's back,' he said.

Rina laughed. Her hands gently touched both sides of his face and then moved down to his fingers, which she placed on her hips. She pressed closer. He found that it was impossible to move without entangling himself even further in her embrace.

She stepped abruptly away. 'I know you are good friends with Garth. Perhaps you are gay?'

'I am adequately heterosexual, although I am not going to prove the point right now.'

'Most men find me very interesting when it comes to intimate encounters.'

'Skee is just down the hall in the gym.'

'He wouldn't dare come in here unannounced. Take off your clothes.'

'Damn it all, Rina! Will you stop it?'

She smiled and again narrowed the distance between them. 'Your resolve has about run down, right?'

'Wrong. I love my wife.'

'Who said that sex had anything to do with marriage?'

'Why are you playing this game, Rina? You've got a younger partner who is probably strong enough to break me in half.'

'And a stupid male. Skee is useful, but without will or resolve, which makes his conquest trivial.' The enigmatic smile that haunted Lyon returned when she cocked her head. 'You are physically afraid of Skee. Yes, of course. That's the reason for your hesitation.'

All things considered, Lyon felt that exhibiting a wide streak of cowardice to this neurotically seductive woman would be the best possible alternative. 'You are right,' he snapped. 'I don't intend to become the strangled hypotenuse in a messy love triangle.'

'Skee always does exactly as I tell him. If I say that you and I are lovers, he will merely shrug and turn away.'

'I'm not anxious to test that sort of loyalty,' Lyon said. 'But I would like to ask you both about the night of Morgan's murder.'

'There's nothing to ask. After we left your place, we returned here and made love. That couch converts, and we slept here.

It went on all night, Lyon. The man was an insatiable stallion until he met me.'

'Then he's bound to remember the night, isn't he?'

'Why don't we go ask him?' Rina said as she petulantly slipped into a robe and sandals.

The gym door was locked. 'It's never locked,' Rina said as she pounded on the door. 'Open the damn door, Skee!'

'He might have gone out,' Lyon said.

'Not without telling me, he wouldn't. I'll get the master key.' She ran to her office and hurried back carrying a large key ring. She fumbled through eight or nine keys until she located the one that opened the gym's door.

It was dark inside the room until Rina flicked several buttons on the panel switch near the door. Three fluorescent lights positioned over the floor-length mirrors on the far wall flickered on. The hulking shadows of exercise machines cast bar patterns across the aisle that led down the center of the room.

Lyon saw Skee prone on a bench press in front of the mirrors. His hands were curled over a barbell holding two hundred pounds of weight. If Lyon hadn't known the room had been dark until seconds ago, he would assume that Skee had momentarily paused before attempting the heavy lift.

'Something's wrong,' Rina said as they started toward Skee. She began to run. 'Something is very wrong!' She reached the bench ahead of Lyon and knelt next to her lover before she screamed.

Lyon put his hands on her shoulders and pulled her away. Rina buried her head in his shoulder. Lyon saw the dead face reflected in the mirrors that ran the length of the wall. There was no way to avoid the swollen features of the prone body-builder stretched out on the bench. His hands were curled over the heavy barbell that lay across his neck. It was apparent that in addition to crushing the windpipe and causing asphyxiation, the weight must have squeezed the carotid arteries and closed the blood supply to the brain.

It had taken Skee a minute to die. The contorted face guaranteed that it had been a painful time.

Eleven

Rina sat stiffly on the seat of an exercise machine. She gazed blankly ahead with the haunted look of a combat-weary soldier's 1,000-yard stare. Lyon wondered if she were in shock, although her respirations seemed to be within normal limits. He decided she was well enough to leave for a few minutes and hurried from the gym to the phone in her office-apartment. He dialed 911 and requested a police and medical examiner response before returning to the gym.

'The police and emergency units will be here shortly,' he told her.

One shoulder shifted slightly in a nearly imperceptible acknowledgment. He watched her for a few moments before he began a search of the area. The exercise room was square and windowless with a single entrance. He threw additional light switches on the panel by the door until a series of flores-cent ceiling fixtures flickered on and bathed the room in a harsh, bright light. On the right of the center aisle were rows of skeletal exercise machines. Stationary bikes lined the left. The floor-to-ceiling mirrors on the far wall did not relieve the room's harsh black and white texture. The exit door did not have an interior lock or handles and was opened by a push plate. It could only be locked from the outside.

Rina muttered something indistinguishable. 'What did you say?' Lyon asked.

Words finally burst from her in a staccato delivery. 'I want it out of here. I want that body out of my place!'

'That will be taken care of as soon as the assistant medical examiner makes a preliminary examination.'

'I do not like dead things. I don't want it here.'

'How did the gym door get locked?' he asked.

'Skee was trying to power-lift too much weight. He couldn't handle it. He wasn't able to get the barbell back on the stand. When he lost his grip it fell and crushed his neck.'

Lyon wondered how Skee managed to get into the hall and lock himself in the gym. Her vacant stare had returned and he expected little positive response from any further questions.

Outside the building, a patrol car's screeching halt coincided with the sounds of its dying siren. A door slammed and running footsteps pounded through the health-food store. Patrolman Jamie Martin arrived at the gym carrying the car's shotgun in one hand and an emergency first-aid kit in the other. Lyon considered that these opposing preparations were confused but admirable.

'Where's the victim?' the young patrolman asked with an edge of apprehension.

Lyon nodded toward the rear of the room as he continued his examination of the door. The argument over the corpse began almost immediately.

'Don't touch the victim!' Jamie yelled.

'Get it out of here. I want it gone!' was Rina's harsh reply.

'Stop touching the deceased! This is a police crime scene.'

Lyon suspected the cause of the argument without returning to the exercise room to confront the situation directly. He would just as soon not get involved any further with Rina. He had hoped that Jamie Martin might be able to handle the situation. He wasn't optimistic. Dealing with Rina seemed to require an oblique mental approach rather than rational diplomacy.

A soft shuffling sound followed by yelps from Jamie signaled that the problem had reached a critical mass. Lyon returned to the gym to find Rina dragging the corpse along the floor by its wrist. The exertion had caused her to lose the belt of her robe so that the garment flapped open exposing her remarkable gymnast figure.

Jamie Martin was torn. He knew that duty required that he subdue the woman and take control of the deceased, but such action required that he touch her, a course of action that simultaneously fascinated and repelled him.

114

Rina continued dragging her dead lover toward the hall.

'What in hell's going on here!' Captain Norbert bellowed as two state police trooper corporals rushed down the gym aisle. As the police reinforcements wrestled with Rina in an attempt to handcuff her to one of the exercise machines, they succeeded in knocking her robe completely off her shoulders. 'I asked what in the hell is going on? Good Christ almighty, it's Wentworth! We find another stiff and who is here but Wentworth again. You are around more dead bodies than a funeral director.'

Rina screamed. Norbert and Lyon ran toward the milling group as the athletic woman, a handcuff dangling from one wrist, climbed to the top of an exercise machine. 'Everyone freeze!' Norbert yelled. The two corporals stepped back in embarrassment while Jamie Martin averted his eyes. 'What is this, funny-farm time? Get that woman down from there,' the state police captain demanded.

'These pigs were copping a feel,' Rina yelled as Lyon picked up her robe from the floor.

'We were cuffing her when—' the first corporal began.

'For God's sake, will someone call a woman cop?' Norbert said in exasperation. 'And arrest that woman for interfering with a police officer, public nudity, lewd conduct, and soliciting.'

Rina leapt to the floor with an agile jump and made a dash for the exit. She had almost pushed through the front doors before she was caught and restrained by the troopers. She directed her high-pitched screech at Captain Norbert. 'I know your type! I've been arrested at rock concerts by pigs like you!'

Norbert glared back. 'Well, that's good, lady. There won't be any surprises for you. Get her out of here,' he snapped. 'This is a crime scene. You, Martin, go interview the store clerk.'

Lyon slipped the robe over Rina's shoulders and gently pulled her against his shoulder. She made tiny chirping noises that were soon broken up by sniffles which turned into a quiet, nearly soundless cry. He kept his arm around her as they walked back to the apartment followed at a discreet distance by the two trooper corporals. 'They will take you to the barracks to be booked. While you get dressed, I can phone an attorney for you.'

'Yes, call Willey P. Lynch. He's in Hartford and—'

'I know how to reach him.'

The state police corporals warily watched Rina as Lyon returned to the gym. Doctor Lars Postman, an assistant medical examiner, had arrived with a photographer and a dour-faced duo from the state forensics lab. The technicians scurried around the gym collecting and labeling. Postman was a notoriously cheerful man who affected either a Groucho Marx walk or a James Cagney strut. It was his constant smile, bad jokes, and intrinsic good spirits under the most dire medical circumstances of death that earned him the label of Doctor Laughing Lars.

'He wasn't in that location when we found him,' Lyon said.

Lars Postman widened his eyes and mimed a long cigar puff. 'Oh, really. You going to the hot-air balloon meet in Farmington on the nineteenth, Lyon?'

'I don't know, Lars. I'm just getting acquainted with my cloudhopper and I'm not quite comfortable enough with it for any public flights. We found the body supine on that bench at the end of this aisle in front of the mirrors.' Lyon walked toward the far end of the room with the doctor following. He pointed at the weights resting on their support rack. 'The barbell was across his neck.'

Lars laughed again. 'I never could figure out why you bought that damn cloudhopper balloon. The thing's an accident waiting to happen. If the rats haven't eaten holes in the envelope, why don't you break the old Wobbly II out of mothballs? It's still stored in your barn, isn't it?'

'The body had a barbell on its neck, Lars,' Lyon said in an attempt to get back to the crime.

'That would be consistent with the injuries I have externally observed at this point.' He laughed. 'Hey, if you don't want to fly yourself, how about driving chase car for me? If I can't get you, I'll end up with Grumpy and Sneezy over there,' he said with a wave at the two busy lab techs.

116

Lyon wished that Dr Postman were more interested in the deceased than balloon meets. 'How long has he been dead, Lars?'

'Who?'

'The corpse that you are presently standing next to.'

Lars laughed and continued his examination. 'Did I tell you that I'm thinking of going wicker on my balloon gondola for the Autopsy III? It's the only way to go.'

'Any ideas?'

'Sure, I like wicker because it's traditional,' the doctor responded as he bent to peer into the dead eyes of the body on the floor.

'I meant time of death,' Lyon said.

The doctor reluctantly looked at his thermometer. 'Dropped a degree. We're talking an hour, two at tops. The stomach contents might reveal more when I get into that.' He straightened up and gestured to the waiting ambulance attendants. 'Come on guys, your turn.' The first attendant pushed a gurney down the aisle while the second shook open a body bag.

Dr Postman shook his head as he gathered his instruments. 'I don't know why you want to talk about bodies rather than ballooning, Lyon. You want dead? Come down to my office. We got dozens.' He waved as he followed the body out the door. 'See you at Farmington.'

Lyon returned to the owner's apartment and was relieved to see that Rina was fully dressed in a prim skirt and conservative blouse. She sat defiantly at the small desk. The troopers sat stiffly on the couch. She seemed relieved to see Lyon return.

'I haven't been busted since my groupie days,' Rina said, 'but the pigs don't seem to change. They're the same now as they were then.'

'Who had a key to the gym?' Lyon asked.

'Who gives a damn?' was her answer.

'I do. Keys, Rina. Who?'

'Naturally Skee and I each had a set. Let's see, the guy who does housekeeping and maintenance had another set. The store manager has them too, and there's an extra set around somewhere.'

117

'Who else was in the building early this morning?'

'No one. The store clerk comes in at nine thirty, as does the receptionist. Before nine it's just Skee and me. Is it gone yet? Is his body gone? I have this thing about dead people.'

'The medical examiner just finished and they're taking the body to the ambulance. Who'd want to kill him, Rina?'

'Why are you going on about keys and killing? Skee had an accident. The barbell strangled him. That's all there is to it.'

Lyon was not a weight lifter, but the elementary physics of Skee's last lift seemed obvious. If he couldn't make the lift and realized he was in danger, simply tilting the barbell to one side or the other would carry it away from his neck and crash it to the floor. A safe way out, unless someone was standing behind him pressing down on the bar to prevent it from tilting. 'I don't think it was an accident.'

'Then it was a burglar. Skee caught someone breaking into the building and they killed him.'

'Rob a health-food store early in the morning and murder a man by forcing him to lie on a bench and then putting a barbell across him? I don't think so, Rina. Any other ideas?'

'How the hell should I know?' she said brusquely, with the return of her usual volatility. The state police corporals sitting on the couch were visibly startled. 'What different does it make to you? You were no friend of Skee's. You're not a cop.'

Lyon didn't pursue the matter. A violent argument had erupted in the corridor. Rocco and his brother-in-law seemed constitutionally unable to carry out a conversation in normal tones.

'What in hell are you doing here, Norbie! This is Murphysville! This is my town, not some state satellite where a resident trooper runs things.'

'These cases are obviously interrelated and therefore state business.'

'Related! How the hell would you know? You don't know who's dead here.'

'We monitor your radio, big man.'

'Who the hell talked in the clear?' Rocco bellowed at his

officers. 'Who the hell didn't use land lines for sensitive information? Heads will roll!' Rocco nearly screamed.

The argument moved into the room, but both men, sensing the presence of civilian personnel, lowered their voices.

Captain Norbert pointed a short blunt finger at Rina. 'Book her,' he ordered the corporals.

'Murder two, Captain?' the first one asked.

'Did I order that? Did I even hint at a capital charge? I want her booked for screwing around with a crime scene and resisting. Got that?'

'I'm not going anywhere,' Rina said. 'And the first guy that lays a finger on me gets a knee in the family jewels.'

'Oh, Jesus, we got one of those,' Norbert said in exasperation. 'Cool it, lady. This isn't a protest rally. There's no one to see you, so why are you putting up a fuss?'

'I'm not going and that's all there is to it.'

'We can take her,' a corporal said as he pulled a sap from his rear pocket and slapped it into the palm of his hand.

'Rina, please,' Lyon said. 'Go on and get it over with.'

'A good lawyer will make a great violation of civil rights case on this bust.'

'You think so?' Rina was beginning to look interested.

'Know so,' Rocco said as he casually scanned the room. 'You'll clear a bundle.'

'Thank you, Chief Herbert,' Norbert said. 'Gentlemen, escort the lady to the car.'

'Why didn't you book her for murder?' Rocco asked after the two troopers took Rina from the building. 'She probably killed Morgan for the trust money and Skee was her accomplice. The boyfriend tried a little extortion, which pissed her off, so that's why she knocked him off. You can build one hell of a circumstantial case around that scenario.'

'Except for this little detail,' Norbert said as he pulled a fax from his inside pocket. 'A copy of this came to the barracks this morning and another went to the governor's office. It was sent from the Murphysville public library.'

'The where?' Rocco asked in astonishment.

'Aren't you listening, Herbert? I said it was faxed from the Murphysville library.'

'For Christ's sake, Norbert, that was a rhetorical what,' Rocco said as he snatched the paper and read it aloud. 'The perjurer Morgan was first. His whore the Boston Bimbo was second. Others may also die by the avenging sword of the Brotherhood of Beelzebub.'

Norbert smirked in satisfaction. 'This second message proves we have a terrorist here. I've already called the local FBI field office and asked them to come in on it. Let the Feds handle this baby and we'll both be off the hook. We get to close our files and the Feds take the heat. Neat, huh?'

'You're telling me that some hate group is knocking off people in Murphysville?' Rocco asked.

'Jesus, Rocco. Avenging swords and whores. That kind of crap smacks of terrorist agents.'

'The fax mentioned a Boston bimbo,' Lyon said. 'Is that a loose translation or is a Boston bimbo related to the whore of Babylon?'

'Don't be a wiseguy, Wentworth. They're accepting responsibility. I take that as involvement. Ten to one we get a letter tomorrow concerning the muscleman killed here this morning.'

Over the years, the town of Murphysville experienced periodic coup d'états in its unsuccessful attempt to overthrow the town librarian, Miss Emily Southgate. The participants in these insurrections were usually dedicated genre readers who objected to Miss Southgate's benign, but authoritarian censorship. Romance novels, westerns, and hardboiled detective mysteries were never purchased or ever catalogued if donated. Miss Southgate, backed by an equally conservative library board, defeated all objections handily.

Emily Southgate squinted over half glasses at Rocco and Lyon as they entered the library. She spoke in the half whisper that through years of use had become her natural voice. 'Those Wobblies of yours are still not acceptable, Mr Wentworth. They are a transparent disguise for the radical IWW. The International Workers of the World were socialists, and you know we do not tolerate that in Murphysville.'

Lyon sighed in resignation over their ancient argument.

'Miss Southgate, can't we just pretend my monsters are benign little guys telling a child's story?'

'I know a parable when I read one. Good day, gentlemen.'

'Ms Southgate,' Rocco said. 'Someone sent a fax from here this morning. Do you know who used the machine today?'

'Two impudent young men from the state police were here earlier asking the same questions. I will give you the same answer that I gave them. No one used that machine this morning, or yesterday morning. Not only have I been at this desk since we opened both days, but there is no notation in the fax log. You gentlemen and the men from the state police were the only people to come in the library today. And that is a sad commentary on the literacy of this town.'

'Where's the machine?' Rocco asked.

'Through that archway. In the reference room by the ency-clopedias. As you can plainly see, no one can get to it without passing by my desk.'

Rocco and Lyon entered the small reference room and found the machine. High shelves hid it from the main desk.

'She's right,' Rocco said. 'It's impossible to get to the machine without crossing by her desk. She said no one came in, and I believe that.'

'And yet we know the message came from this machine, but I doubt that our neighborhood terrorist would make a log entry. What's this door?' Lyon asked as he stepped between two shelves. 'It's unlocked.'

Rocco arched an eyebrow. 'That's interesting. Where does it go?'

Lyon eased the door open and fumbled along the inside wall until he found a light switch. A single bulb halfway down the stairs illuminated a narrow stairwell leading to a basement door. Rocco put a restraining hand on Lyon's shoulder, drew his revolver, and led the way. They opened the door at the bottom of the stairwell and entered a dim room illuminated only by light from narrow windows high on the walls. Clusters of tiny tables surrounded by low shelves holding outsize picture books indicated that they were in the children's room.

The windows in the air-conditioned room were sealed shut. The other door in the room led outside and was securely locked. They returned to Miss Southgate at the front desk.

'Where's the children's librarian?' Rocco asked.

'Phyllis Baxter only works in the afternoons and on Saturdays when school's in session. Obviously the children are not allowed here when they should be in school. She will open at three.'

'But she came in this morning?' Rocco pressed.

'Of course not. Why should she?'

Rocco hung up the phone at Sarge's Bar and returned to the booth shaking his head. 'My guys checked it out. The children's librarian, Phyllis Baxter, definitely did not come into work early today. She has a pretty good alibi.'

'Which is?' Lyon asked.

'She was setting up bingo boards for tonight's game at St Margaret and was seen by Father Leonard, five other women, and a visiting nun.'

'That visiting nun alibi will do it every time,' Lyon said.

'I'm really wondering if Norbie was right to close everything down in favor of some religious fanatical college dropouts.'

'Of course Norbie could be right,' Lyon said. 'But there's also some other strong alternatives. Rina has a unique turn of mind, and under certain circumstances might be capable of killing her half-brother.'

'With Skee's help. Then when he became a problem, she did away with him.'

'Morgan might have let them in the RV later that night and they used his sword to kill him,' Lyon said.

'The same sequence can be applied to Clay and his topless dancer friend. Of all the people we know who were around the RV that night, Bambi probably had the best opportunity to talk Morgan into opening the door. Once inside the RV they disposed of Morgan and attempted to hang it on you. Bambi proceeds to get greedy and Clay does her in. But in that scenario I don't see why Skee would be killed.'

'To make Bambi's death logical,' Lyon said. 'Remember

the so-called letter from the Beelzebubs? Death to the bimbo or whatever. Ten to one there will be another letter acknowledging Skee's death.'

'As a further cover-up.'

Lyon nodded. 'All this conjecture doesn't exclude Ernest or Garth, both of whom had more than enough reason to kill Morgan.'

'Morgan had confidential information on both of them,' Rocco said. 'Did you ever consider the possibility that they protest their hostility too much? Is it possible their mutual antagonism may not be as real as it appears? They could have joined forces to do Morgan in and are using the other two murders as decoys.'

'We did seem to disarm them rather easily. A case could be made that Garth's attempt to shoot Ernest was staged. To make matters more complicated, no one in the whole damn group seems to have a good alibi, and everyone has a motive,' Lyon said.

Rocco began to laugh. 'God, the combinations are endless. How about the killer twins, Rina and Clay, operating without their lovers?'

The black humor was infectious and Lyon laughed. 'Or Bambi and Skee doing the dirty work for payment by the twins? Oh, Lord help us. There are suspects everywhere and what in the hell are we laughing at?'

Rocco kept chuckling until it was time to order another drink.

'Do you have a death wish? Or are you just out to lunch?' Bea asked. 'That thing is not a full-fledged balloon. It is the top half of a hot-air balloon. I would like to point out that it does not have a basket to ride in.'

'Gondola,' Lyon replied.

'Whatever. At least in a regular balloon I have the faint illusion that there's something substantial underneath. In that thing there is nothing at all beneath you.'

Lyon stopped adjusting the flame on the propane burner of the cloudhopper balloon and looked across the yard at his alarmed wife. She seemed more frightened of his impending balloon flight than when she had relieved Garth of his .45 caliber pistol.

He looked up at the thirty-foot-wide 21,000-cubic-foot balloon. It was bobbing a few feet above his head, straining against its tether, which was fastened to a stake in the ground. 'It's perfectly safe, you know. I've been hot-air ballooning for years and this one is just a slightly different version.'

'The bigger ones are bad enough, but this thing is ridiculous. And if you're so damn good, what about the time you landed on the golf course and those men tried to kill you with their putters?'

'They were five-irons actually. Those guys had a lot of money riding on that particular hole.'

'Or the day you dropped in on a nudist camp?'

'I've always liked volley ball.'

'And how many times have you dunked in the Connecticut River? That thing is dangerous. Can you be tempted not to go?'

'Nope. Care to come with me? I can hold you in my arms.'

'I wouldn't go up in that thing for all the whatever they have in China these days. As for you, everyone has a price.' Bea closed the distance between them and slipped her arms around his neck. She gently moved the rucksack-like frame containing the propane burner with her feet. 'You were great in the laurel,' she said. 'How would you like to be bedded in the begonias?'

Lyon kissed her and moved the propane burner further away with his foot. Air began to cool inside the balloon, which caused it to bob toward the ground.

'Go for it, man!' a voice behind them yelled.

Lyon and Bea snapped apart to stare toward the construction site. The tower crane had been moved to the near edge of their property and the operator in the high cab leaned out the window to wave at them. 'You two are better than an adult video store.'

'Oh, my God! He watched us in the mountain laurel,' Bea said as she ran toward the house in embarrassment.

'Come on back here, it's show time,' the crane operator yelled after her. He looked back at the sinking balloon to see a furious Lyon Wentworth stalking across the lawn toward the construction site. He slammed and locked the cab windows and swivelled the crane arm to lift another steel girder.

Lyon saw that the voyeuristic crane operator had buttoned up his cab and would be impossible to reach. He walked back to the cloudhopper and let his anger at the workman merge with his general dislike of the whole condominium project.

He centered the propane burner under the balloon's envelope and gave it a ten-second burn to reheat the interior air and restore balance to the balloon. He slipped into the parachute-type harness and adjusted the rucksack containing the propane burner. After the mooring line was released, he pulled the short lanyard to give the burner another five seconds of fire. The last burn changed the balloon's equilibrium and he was snatched aloft as the balloon bobbed quickly above the trees.

A light wind from the northeast carried him away from the construction site and Nutmeg Hill and along the westerly bank of the river. The balloon rose slowly after its initial surge for altitude. He nursed it slightly higher until it stabilized at eight hundred feet above the river.

Lyon hung suspended from the harness as the wind carried the balloon slowly forward. The sense of freedom that balloon flight always gave him began to form as the noiseless journey continued. He rocked gently in the harness and occasionally shattered the silence with the barking whoosh of an additional propane burn to keep the flight level.

He recalled a free-fall parachute jump he had made years ago. Before the canopy opened there was a fleeting moment when he had experienced this exhilaration. Balloon flight was an extension of such feelings. He often imagined that he saw the slowly moving panorama of the land below in the same manner as a large bird whose sweeping glides banked at the whim of warm air currents.

These flights were an excellent time for reflection. They were so far removed from ordinary surroundings that the mind seemed to view problems in a different manner. Lyon often felt that the subconscious mind could worry a seemingly unsolvable problem like a silent terrier dog. If a solution or part of a solution were reached, it would often be fed back to the conscious mind. It was necessary to create the breeding ground and receptivity for this type of oblique thought.

The balloon was nearly out of its hour-long supply of propane before the answer came. It was then that he knew who had sent the fax from the town library and delivered the letter to the police station. The solution to those two questions would lead them to the zealots.

Lyon Wentworth impatiently pulled the ripping panel to release hot air from the balloon envelope. The spilled air caused the craft to begin a rapid descent. He was unable to change direction in any manner, and his only control was the ability to adjust the rate of descent by heating air with the propane burner. If he continued on his present landing course, he was going to land on the Murphysville town green, which seemed preferable to snagging the steeple of the Congregational Church.

Twelve

He had vented the balloon too early. The wind had suddenly shifted during his descent toward the town green. This reverse changed his horizontal drift and swept him toward the buildings lining the green's north border. He had planned a stepped approach with a gradual loss of altitude until he hovered over the lawn near the gazebo. At that point he intended to touch down gently for a stand-up landing. This was not to be.

The wind carried him at tree-top level toward the classical New England Congregational Church situated at the edge of the green.

When the sagging envelope cleared the pointed steeple, he had renewed hopes of a safe but jarring landing in the empty parking lot behind the church. The suspension harness snagged on the steeple point. The abrupt halt spilled the remaining hot air from the bag and slammed him against the side of the building, where he hung against the belfry.

He was never sure whether the shock of his body hitting against the belfry or an irate custodian were the cause. The church clarion began blaring a version of 'Onward Christian Soldiers' from a gigantic speaker that was aimed directly at him.

Halfway down the block the door to Ernest Harnell's house burst open. The alarmed English professor rushed outside carrying a 30.06 rifle with a mounted telescopic sight at port arms. He stopped abruptly in the center of the street and stared up at the steeple in astonishment.

Ernest slung the rifle over his shoulder. He walked closer to the building as the clarion mercifully stopped.

'Are you invading the town, Wentworth? Or do you just like the view from up there?'

'*Call the fire department!*' Lyon yelled loudly, still half deafened by 'Christian Soldiers'.

'I was working at my desk when I looked out my window to see what looked like a paratrooper invasion. Reminded me of World War Two when Papa and his band of French resistance fighters liberated Paris.' He unslung the rifle and wrapped the sling around his forearm as he raised the scope to his eye and drew a bead on the helpless man hanging from the steeple. 'God, what an easy shot.'

'Don't point that thing at me! Damn it, Ernest! I mean it!' Lyon heard two sets of approaching sirens and then the deep whistle blast from the volunteer firehouse.

'I might play God and decide if you live or die . . .' Ernest squeezed the trigger and the bolt snapped on an empty chamber.

A patrol car swerved to a stop and Rocco catapulted from the driver's seat and rushed toward Ernest. 'Give me that goddamn weapon.'

'Hell, no! This is an expensive piece.' The teacher's voice rose three registers in high-pitched protest.

Rocco snatched the rifle. 'I'm having the state lab run a test on this.' He placed the weapon in the trunk of the patrol car and walked back to the steeple with a bullhorn. 'You know what this means, Wentworth.' Rocco Herbert's voice echoed over the green. 'The volunteer fire department is going to have to crank out the hook and ladder, and they are going to be pissed.'

It was another five minutes before the extension ladder began to slowly rise from its truck bed and swing toward the steeple.

'Crimminy nicket, Wentworth,' Volunteer Fire Chief Terry Randall said. He was perched near the top of the ladder as it hovered over the church. He hooked his safety harness to the rail. 'We voted last year that we wouldn't do kittens anymore. This year I'm putting a ban on balloonists.' He was perched near the top of the ladder as it hovered over the church. 'You know, I got a guy waiting in my barber chair. When he finishes leafing through my *Playboy* he's going to get restless. That's when he's going to start thinkin'' on the new unisex shop on Essex Street with the young women stylists.'

'Sorry about that, Chief.'

'If I didn't think so damn much of Senator Wentworth, you'd stay up here until they replaced you with the Star of Bethlehem at Christmastime.'

When Lyon was able to shift his weight to the ladder and release the harness, the balloon envelope fell free and drifted down to the parking lot. With Rocco's help he rolled up the deflated balloon and stuffed it into the back of the patrol car. By the time the balloon was secure, the fire engine had pulled away and Ernest had disappeared into his house.

'We'll celebrate another of your safe landings at Sarge's, where I can write up your summons,' Rocco said.

Lyon shook his head. 'I'd like to talk with Mrs Baxter.'

Rocco looked puzzled. 'The children's librarian?'

'Do you know where she lives?'

'Sure. Not far from here over on Webb Street.'

'Did you ever develop any information from the middle-school principal about the kid who delivered the letter to police headquarters?' Lyon asked.

'Nothing. Either we had a bad lead or he's a stubborn kid who won't admit anything.'

'Let's see what Mrs Baxter has to say.'

'I told you she has an cast-iron alibi. At the time the fax was sent from the library, she was with the visiting nun. Remember?'

'I recall.'

Phyllis Baxter was neat. The narrow lawn of the small ranch house was well trimmed and edged. The compact car squatting under the carport gleamed, and the tiny living room was immaculate. Mrs Baxter was coordinated with her surroundings, which meant that her essence could be summarized as scrubbed and shining. Lyon recalled that half a dozen years ago her husband, a maintenance worker for the light company, had been accidentally electrocuted. That was not a neat way to expire.

She had been widowed with a young child before her thirtieth birthday, but had met the situation with determination and resolution.

She looked down at the small Timex watch on her wrist. 'I only have a minute, Chief Herbert. I open the children's room at three.'

'We're trying to track down who sent a fax from the library,' Rocco said.

'Yes, I know. One of your men talked with me earlier today. I told him I was at the church annex this morning and haven't been in the library since yesterday afternoon.'

'The first job I ever had was shelving books at the Middleburg Library,' Lyon said. 'I did it after school three afternoons a week.'

Unable to follow the trail of Lyon's thought, Rocco frowned.

Phyllis Baxter returned an even smile. 'Miss Southgate allows me to indulge in a little nepotism. I've hired my son to shelve in the children's section. But since Murphysville is such a small town, he's only required to work two afternoons a week.'

'It must be a great comfort to have your son helping,' Lyon said. 'You must be very proud of him.'

'I am. Since Big Ralph died, little Ralph has tried so hard to take his place. We make do with social security, a small pension from the light company, and the little I make at the library. It's a tight budget, but we manage. In addition to his two afternoons a week at the library, Ralphie delivers the *Hartford Courant* in the morning and the *Middleburg Press* in the afternoon. He is always looking out for ways to make money and help out.'

Rocco began to look interested. 'Does his paper route include the police station?'

'No, it doesn't. But he often substitutes for the delivery girl who has that route.'

'And he has a key to the children's room?' Lyon asked.

'Of course, but he's completely trust— What are you suggesting?'

'I think we had better talk to your son,' Rocco said.

The New England formality that was this woman's protective mantle against the world stiffened at the faintest suggestion of any wrongdoing by her son. Her body imperceptibly tensed as her knees pressed firmly together. 'He has chores to do,' was her cool reply.

Rocco sounded tired. 'I think today's first chore is to speak with me.'

'I think not, Chief Herbert. My son is not involved in any criminal activity, and I do not want him hounded and frightened.'

'I didn't say it was criminal, Mrs Baxter. Now, are you going to let me talk with him or do I have to have him picked up by a patrol car?'

Little Ralph Baxter was nearly as neat as Phyllis Baxter. He sat rigidly on the couch in the small living room next to his mother. He was a smallish, tow-headed, twelve-year-old, and appeared mildly anxious as he sensed the tenseness transmitted by his mother.

Phyllis Baxter put her hand over her son's. 'You must tell Chief Herbert exactly what you've been doing, Ralphie.'

'I haven't done anything wrong, Mom.'

'Did you go to the library this morning and send a message on the fax machine?' Rocco asked.

'I was in school this morning,' was the too quick response.

'During your morning paper route you had to ride your bike past the library. You went inside using your own key and sent a message.'

'No, sir,' was the prompt and polite response.

Phyllis Baxter abruptly stood and stepped in front of her son as if to shield him from further attack. It was the simple and reflexive act of an animal mother protecting her young. 'All right, that's it. You can't badger my son any further. He told you he didn't do anything.'

'Tell them about the fingerprints on the fax machine, Rocco,' Lyon said. It was a necessary lie at this juncture.

Ralphie Baxter blanched as Rocco solemnly spoke. 'I'm afraid we'll have to take him down to the station and book him in order to get his prints. He shouldn't be in the juvenile detention center for more than a week or two . . . unless the social workers step in, and you know how they are.'

The woman's fingers curled into tight fists that pressed fearfully against her face. 'No,' was her nearly inaudible response.

Lyon looked at the stricken young boy and nodded. The look and gesture were command enough.

'I should have said something when they were asking around school,' Ralphie said. 'I was afraid they'd want me to give the money back. I knew something was bad wrong cuz he was paying me so much for hardly doing anything. I figured something was probably wrong with what I was doing, even though he said it was a practical joke.'

'What were you doing, Ralphie?' Rocco asked gently.

'Once I delivered an envelope to police headquarters, and early this morning I sneaked into the library and sent a fax. He paid me twenty dollars each time. He said it was a joke he was pulling on some people. But I knew something was wrong.'

'Tell me,' Rocco said. 'Exactly how did you meet this man?'

On the last stop of his afternoon paper route, Ralphie Baxter delivered four copies of the *Middleburg Press* to the Acorn Motel. His daily routine, after he dropped the papers off at the motel office, was to buy a Pepsi from the machine in the center stairwell. Several days ago he had dropped coins in the machine, waited for the can to thunk to a stop at the end of the chute, and then popped its top. He was startled by a voice from the stairs behind him and nearly dropped the cold can.

'Hey, kid,' the voice from the man halfway down the stairs said. 'You want to earn a couple of bucks?'

He could only see the bottom half of the man on the stairs. 'I got a paper route.'

'I'm talking easy money, kid.'

Ralphie glanced at his bike leaning against the wall not five feet away, and beyond that he could see the motel office only a few feet away. His mother had repeatedly warned him about men who offered money or gifts for small favors. He knew he was supposed to run away and call the police, or at least pedal quickly home or to the library on his ten-speed.

A twenty-dollar bill fluttered down the stairs and gently landed on the concrete floor near Ralphie's feet. 'That's for doing practically nothing, kid. I want you to deliver a letter for me. Simple enough? It's a joke I'm pulling.'

'That's all?'

'Promise.' A hand appeared and flicked an envelope at Ralphie's feet. When he picked it up he saw that it was addressed to the Murphysville Police Department.

'What do I have to do?'

'Take it to the cops and leave it at the front desk. Don't talk to anyone. When you come back tomorrow we may have another little well-paying errand for you. This is all top-secret joke stuff, you know? So keep it quiet or the money stops.'

'I don't have to do anything else?'

'Nothing.'

It seemed harmless enough. Ralphie stuffed the envelope in his back pocket. After all, the letter was going to the police station, so what could be wrong with that?

The request to send the fax had been handled the same way.

It was after the first delivery that Ralphie's Junior Achievement mind began to churn. His timid suggestion to his benefactor concerning increased distribution of his 'joke' was accepted readily with a reward payment of an additional twenty. The first fax message had been easy, and the man at the motel promised that there might be others, each one bearing an additional twenty.

Rocco Herbert slouched in the passenger side of the Dodge pickup and cleaned the lens of his binoculars with his shirt tail. 'I am probably the only peace officer in the entire country whose unmarked vehicle is a twelve-year-old borrowed pickup with a rusted body carrying a hot-air balloon.'

'Don't you think you should call Norbie and let him bring a state police SWAT team out here?' Lyon said. 'This guy is very dangerous.'

'Let's see what we're up against first,' Rocco replied as he raised the glasses and swept the second tier of the Acorn Motel.

'When do you get the ballistics results on Ernest's rifle?'

'We don't,' Rocco responded without removing his eyes from the lens.

'Wrong caliber?'

'When I got back to headquarters the gun wasn't in the car.'

'Ernest took it while the ladder was getting me down?'

'He denies it and says a small crowd gathered to watch the festivities and anyone could have taken it. He says he's going to sue me for the cost of the rifle. As if I didn't have enough problems. It probably won't make any difference if this is the guy we want.'

'What do you see?' Lyon asked as Rocco continued staring at the motel's upper units.

'Not a damn thing.'

'Maybe he's not here,' Lyon said.

'According to the motel manager, there's only three units that have been rented continuously this week. Two of those rooms are occupied by single mothers with children, whose charges are paid by the welfare department. The third is rented to what he calls a weird guy who hardly ever goes out. He checked in the night before Morgan was killed.'

'That sounds solid,' Lyon said.

'Uh huh,' Rocco replied. He swept the upper tier of the motel again with the binoculars. 'Now, let's figure out how we're going to take this guy.'

The intention was to blow the bitch to hell. It must be certain that there would be enough high explosives in the bomb to completely destroy the car. The initial explosion would disintegrate the vehicle into twisted metal shards. Hopefully there would be enough additional force for her body to be hurled

134

a hundred feet. That little involuntary aerial event would guarantee that there was no possibility of her survival.

There were no more risks to be taken. Care and protection were the new bywords. A remote bomb, unsatisfactory as it might be, would have to suffice.

The device was a model of simplicity, which made it easy to construct. The dynamite was stolen from the construction site next to the Wentworths' home. The detonating caps had been purchased out of state. The complete bundle would be wrapped in heavy tape and inserted under her car hood, where it would be wired to the starter motor. When the bitch turned the ignition, the car battery would send a spark of electricity to the starter motor and ignite the cap. The resulting explosion would flip off the hood and push the engine block back through the fire wall into the lap of the driver. Her body would be flung back through the rear of the car. There should be sufficient force to expel her either through the shattered rear window or right through the car roof. Her body would pinwheel through the air in a disjointed awkward dance until it fell to the ground with all the grace of a dead bird.

It would be a glorious sight. Pity that it would not be seen.

Lyon Wentworth sometimes viewed terrain in a military manner. This habit annoyed him for two reasons: his brief military career had been in intelligence and not as a line officer, and he preferred to avoid war-like emotional baggage. Nevertheless, the trait often popped up unbidden and he found himself considering fields of fire, possible avenues of concealment, and potential flanking movements. As he sat in his rusting pickup, next to an absorbed Rocco Herbert, he found himself viewing their objective in such a manner.

The Acorn Motel was set twenty yards back from the highway and built in an L which partially surrounded a swimming pool and patio. Bright yellow stucco disguised cement-block construction. A large neon Acorn on the roof also welcomed salesmen. The second tier of rooms was reached by a central stairwell whose enclosure contained an ice machine and soft-drink dispenser.

The room nearest the top of the center stairs was occupied by a man identified by the manager as, 'the guy who paid cash for a week in advance and talks in twenty-five dollar words.'

'You'll want marksmen deployed on the roof and also positioned over by those trees,' Lyon said. 'You'll need men covering the front and rear, and hopefully you can infiltrate the surrounding units and clear the area. When everyone's in place, there are two ways to go in. Either have men repel off the roof and swing through the unit's front picture window, or else use stun grenades followed by a frontal assault behind a battering ram. A command post can be set up in an unmarked van parked down the highway around the curve, and—'

'Nope,' Rocco said sharply to cut him off.

'You want your command post in the motel office?'

'Nope means no troops, I'm taking this guy myself.'

'That's only not necessary, it's poor police procedure, and happens to be against your own back-up rules. This guy may be a trained terrorist, which means that you are around the bend if you consider anything less than a maximum effort.'

'You'll cover me,' Rocco said. 'That should be adequate.' He reached under the seat to retrieve the .12-gauge shotgun he'd placed there when they'd changed vehicles. He worked the pump to throw a shell into the chamber. 'You don't even have to aim.' he said. 'So we won't need your vaunted marksman's eye. Try and not blow away any civilians or me when I'm in your line of fire.'

Lyon reluctantly grasped the weapon by its pistol grip. 'I'm not sure about the legality of this.'

'If we succeed, no one will ask,' Rocco said. 'If we don't, it won't really matter to either of us.'

'That instills a great deal of confidence in me,' Lyon said.

They drove the pickup two hundred yards further down the highway to the entrance of a graveled road. Another quarter of a mile down the side road and they started across a fallow field with the truck groaning and creaking at each jounce of the uneven surface. They parked behind an unused barn near the motel and ran in a crouch to the side of the building's windowless wall.

Rocco pressed against the stucco as he slowly worked his way toward the rear of the units. When he reached the end of the building, he knelt on one knee to peer around the corner. He motioned for Lyon to join him and whispered, 'It's clear. We're going up the stairs. The unit next to his is vacant and I have a master key. I'm going in that way and will break through the connecting door. You'll cover the front of his room and block any escape route from that direction.'

'What about windows?'

'There's only two. A small one in the bathroom at the rear, but it's too small for anyone to squeeze through. The second is the picture window with the drawn drapes next to the front door. You'll be able to cover both the door and window.'

Lyon nodded. 'Got it.'

'OK. In exactly four minutes I break through the connecting door.' Rocco looked at the wide diver's watch strapped to his wrist. 'At the mark the time is exactly—'

'I'm not wearing a watch,' Lyon said.

'Damn it, Wentworth! How am I going to make a raid if you can't synchronize your watch with me?'

'To be honest, Rocco, when I left the house this morning I didn't exactly dress for an attack against a Brother of Beelzebub.'

Rocco sighed. 'We'll have to make do. I'll break through in three minutes. Count it off mentally or something. Just be at that front door when I need you.'

Lyon nodded again as Rocco left. He waited for what he estimated to be a minute and a half and then rushed around the corner and climbed the steps two at a time. At the top of the landing he pressed against the wall in the narrow space between the unit's front door and the wide picture window with its drawn drapes. He continued his internal count while tightly gripping the shotgun.

Wood splintered inside the motel room. 'Freeze, you son-of-a-bitch! Police!'

A woman screamed.

'Damn it!' Rocco yelled. 'Get away from her! I'm warning you, get away!'

As Lyon reached for the door knob to go to Rocco's aid,

the picture window behind him shattered. A man entangled in the window drape smashed though the glass and rolled across the walk. Lyon spun around and raised the shotgun to a firing position.

The man rolled out of the drape and sprang to his feet holding an Uzi in both hands. The assault weapon's barrel swept toward Lyon.

Lyon's finger tightened against the trigger as he pointed the shotgun at the man's head.

'I'll shoot you,' the man with the Uzi said, 'and I'll cut you in half.'

Lyon's instant of supremacy passed. That single golden moment when his weapon dominated the situation disappeared. Each man held a weapon aimed at the other. Each was capable of killing the other. It was probable that involuntary muscle contractions could cause either of them, although shot dead, to fire and kill the other.

'Drop it,' the other man said.

The shotgun clattered to the cement walkway. The man pressed the assault weapon's short barrel against Lyon's neck.

Inside the unit, Rocco ripped the latch chain from the door and threw it open.

'Make funny moves and your partner dies,' said the man.

'Put your hands behind your head and lie face down on the concrete,' Rocco said as he assumed a shooting stance.

'You do not understand,' the man replied. 'Make another move and I will fire. At this range your friend's head will explode.'

Rocco shook his head. 'You're the one who needs to understand. I don't give a damn about him. I need you and it doesn't matter if you are alive or dead. In fact, it's neater if you're dead. I am going to kill you in three seconds.'

Lyon was surprised at the conviction in his friend's voice. 'I believe him,' he said.

'I believe him too,' the man with the Uzi said as his weapon clattered to the walk.

A woman appeared in the doorway behind Rocco. Lyon recognized her as Lorretta Bing, who worked at the motel as a chambermaid and who also supplied some of the male customers with more than just linen. 'Does this mean the party's over, Winston?' she asked petulantly.

Thirteen

Winston Crawford was sullen as he sat on the cracked leather couch in Rocco's office. His arms were handcuffed in front of him and the cuffs were manacled to a metal waistband. He glared at Rocco. 'This arrest might add to your glory, Herbert, but I'm getting screwed to the wall.'

'When I'm through with your list of charges,' Rocco said, 'you'll be part of the wall.'

'I've seen you somewhere before,' Lyon said. 'Weren't you a graduate student at Middleburg University?'

'An adjunct teacher without a future,' Winston replied. 'Thanks to the way Professor Morgan sabotaged my application for a full-time position. His well-chosen words gave the death sentence to my academic future.'

'And you'd really kill to avenge a bad college reference?'

'It's about time these so-called intellectuals took the disenfranchised seriously. We mean to make the world pay attention to the abuse of power.' Lyon realized that the man's thwarted intellect had honed him into an instrument of hatred.

Patrolman Jamie Martin grunted as he carried in a large cardboard box that clanked when he lowered it to the desk in front of Rocco. 'This is heavy stuff, Chief,' he said. 'And there's more to come.'

Rocco nodded an acknowledgment as he began to carefully remove objects from the box and neatly align them across the desk. 'We confiscated this little collection from Crawford's motel room and van,' he said to Lyon. 'Look at this crap. Hand grenades.' He held one up. 'You have your choice: percussion, smoke, or phosphorus.' He shook his head. 'Six automatic pistols, including a Glock, army .45 and Magnum .44. There's enough ammunition for a small war of indeterminate length and knives in assorted sizes. God only knows what else that we haven't inventoried yet.'

'How about this baby, Chief?' Jamie Martin said as he re-entered the room carrying an M60 machine gun in both arms. Belts of ammunition crisscrossed his chest like a Mexican bandit. 'Found it stowed under a blanket in the van.' He stood the machine gun in the corner and draped bands of ammunition over a file cabinet.

'Jesus, Winston,' Rocco said. 'Did you intend to line us up on the green and annihilate the town?'

'I'm a collector,' the manacled man said.

'Obviously, and you're having a going-out-of-business sale.'

'Why do you anarchists always seem to get baby carriages in the line of fire?' Lyon asked.

'Because they don't give a damn who gets in the way,' Rocco said.

'You think your badge gives you indemnity for hypocrisy. An hour ago you were perfectly willing to let me blow your friend's head off in order to capture me for your own glory.' He grimaced at Lyon. 'How do you like being cannon fodder?'

'I suppose it's possible to consider the situation Rocco faced as a problem in game theory,' Lyon said. 'I'm sure he evaluated the alternatives. If you shot me, he shot you. If he didn't shoot you, you might kill both of us. If he hadn't done what he did, the question was, would you have fired? The situation dictated that you would. Rocco took the only course of action available that might save everyone's life.'

'If any man had sacrificed me like that, I would never rest until he died.'

'If there are any sacrificial lambs in this room, you're the only one bleating,' Rocco said. 'Suppose we get a steno-grapher in here to take down your confession? I'd like to hear all the lowdown on this Armageddon crap.'

'Not much to kick around, Chief. I wrote a few letters and then basked in the bloody limelight. I couldn't have asked for better circumstances, starting with a death by sword.'

'You could look at it that way,' Rocco said with good

141

humor. 'Let's see, you knocked off Morgan, the dancer Bambi, and now Skee. You did do Skee, didn't you?'

'Ski who?'

'The bodybuilder. The musclebound friend of Rina's?'

'If he's connected to Morgan, I did him. I'll get a letter off as soon as I learn the details. I'll do that first thing in the morning, if you'd like.'

'A simple confession should be enough.'

Winston shrugged. 'I hope you liked my letters. I tried to work in the proper attitude.'

'They had a rather bloodthirsty ring to them,' Rocco said.

'I was really quite lucky to arrive here and find Morgan already dead. Of course I took the credit. When the woman died, it was bonus time. They seem to be dropping like flies around here.'

Rocco's chair rocked forward as his benign smile faded. 'What in the hell are you talking about?'

'I really fell into a good thing here. I came to do Morgan and I turned up roses.'

'You didn't kill Morgan?' Lyon asked.

'What do you mean, he didn't murder Morgan?' Rocco yelled.

'I'm going to confess, of course,' Winston said. 'And you've got all these weapons. I assume you'll plant the ballistics evidence on me, and maybe I could help you phony the fingerprints? It will do nothing but put the spotlight on Middleburg University's abuse of power.'

'Are you trying to create an insanity defense here, Crawford? Doing in a professor who blighted your college job application? I'm asking you once more,' Rocco said. 'Did you kill those people?'

'Of course not. I merely took the credit. It was rather convenient to get all the glory without having to do the bloody work. The beauty of it all was that the real killer didn't seem to mind.'

'I do not believe this is the man who attacked me with the sword,' Lyon said. 'An attempt was made to frame me and implicate him. Someone else killed those people.'

Rocco catapulted to his feet with a velocity that slammed

the desk chair back against the wall. 'We've been had! While we've been fooling around with this clown, the perp is getting away.'

Winston took a quick step across the room and bent forward so that his manacled hands could snatch a fragmentation hand grenade from the desk. He retreated clutching the weapon. 'I might be a number of things, Chief, but I am not a clown! Get on the floor before we're all blown to hell.' He pulled the grenade's pin but continued to clamp the lever against its body so that it did not pop off and complete the arming. 'Back off!'

'Give me that damn thing!' Rocco said as he reached for Winston's hands.

The defrocked intellectual released his grip on the lever, which immediately spun off the grenade and allowed the striker to hit the cap and activate the four-second fuse.

'For anarchy!' he screamed as he gripped the live grenade.

'For Lyon!' Rocco answered as he snatched the grenade from the man's fingers and flipped it over his shoulder.

'For the hole!' Lyon yelled as he scooped the grenade from the air. He turned without looking and rammed his hand through the closed window. He released the live hand grenade outside into a cellar window receptacle as they all dropped to the floor. The grenade exploded at the furnace-room window below ground level. Several pieces of shrapnel ricocheted up through the flooring, missed the three prone men, and buried themselves in the ceiling.

Bea Wentworth was extremely angry. She stood in front of Rocco's desk with her fingers curled over two .30-caliber ammunition boxes which she occasionally thumped together to emphasize a point.

Lyon sat on the couch nursing his hand. Crawford had been thrown into a cell.

'This is a confrontation not a discussion, Rocco,' Bea said as she thumped an ammunition box.

'The guy was on a mission of revenge and grabbed a hand grenade,' Rocco said with a shrug. 'You have to expect that

143

sort of behavior when a man gets thrown out of the ivory tower.'

'Come on!' Bea said. 'You allowed an unguarded prisoner in the office a few feet away from live weapons. And he almost blew you both up. Suppose someone had been in the yard when Lyon dropped that bomb out the window?'

'We expect risks in police work,' Rocco said without a great deal of conviction.

'You both went into that motel room after an armed man without proper back-up.'

'Damn it all, Bea! The circumstances dictated that.'

'You would not allow your brother-in-law any credit on the bust,' Bea said.

'Now that I remember,' Lyon said. 'Three years ago you fired Jake Manly for going into a convenience store during an armed robbery without calling for back-up.'

'Lyon is not a sworn police officer,' Bea said. 'He is not even an auxiliary constable. He is a civilian.'

'I seem to substitute as the town's bomb-disposal squad,' Lyon said.

Captain Norbert of the state police, flanked by his two-corporal entourage, erupted into the room. His glare encompassed everyone but settled on Lyon with particular distaste. 'I understand you detonated a bomb within the Murphysville city limits?'

'In a manner of speaking,' Lyon answered.

'That's against several laws, Wentworth, or do you effete intellectuals bother about such things?'

'The hand-grenade perpetrator is in cell two,' Rocco snapped. 'He claims he didn't kill anyone and only took the credit to highlight the so-called plight of the anarchists.'

'I believe him,' Lyon added.

'Of course he didn't do it. That's what they all say. If he didn't kill the bodybuilder, do you expect me to believe that our lady gymnast put a two-hundred-pound weight on the guy's neck?'

'She had enough strength to take the same weight off his neck when she decided to move the body. There are other suspects who are also capable,' Lyon said.

'You are a civilian and you are not a law officer, thank God.'

'I'm afraid the proof will be when the next victim dies,' Lyon said.

Lyon and Bea stood outside the Murphysville police station as Jamie Martin's patrol car slid to a halt behind Bea's parked compact. The young patrolman came toward them and gave Bea a short salute. 'Good evening, Senator. They fixed your car while you were inside.'

'There's nothing wrong with my car.'

Jamie shrugged. 'A guy in coveralls and a baseball cap pulled up in a van and popped the hood on your car. He only worked under there a couple of minutes before he slammed it shut and drove off. So maybe it was a mistake.'

'Probably,' Bea said as she retrieved car keys from her pocketbook. She slid behind the wheel.

For a brief moment Lyon felt a chill. He had an inchoate sense of dimming of sunlight and the fluttering of an unknown fear. He drove the thought from his mind. The car was parked directly in front of the town police station in full view of the dispatcher's console. It would be impossible for anything to be wrong.

'It's beginning to rain,' he said as she reached for the ignition.

'Good for the plants,' Bea replied.

'It's going to fall on my balloon in the back of the pickup and it's hard for me to manage with this hand. Would you drive?'

'We certainly wouldn't want our balloon to get wet,' she said as she left her car and went to the pickup in the parking lot.

Dark rain clouds obscured the sky and rain began to fall as they pulled away from the police services building in Lyon's twelve-year-old pickup truck. Bea had to lean slightly forward on the seat to peer through the windshield. The creaking wipers swept an uneven swatch in their losing battle against the heavy rain.

'How's your hand?' she asked without turning her attention away from the misting road.

145

'Not bad.' He worked his fingers back and forth with a slight wince. 'It'll be all right tomorrow.'

'I haven't been to the supermarket. This damn case has me running all over the state getting information. We'll find something in the freezer to throw into the microwave unless you want to eat out.' Bea leaned further forward as the rain continued its incessant beat against the roof and windows of the truck.

'Freezer luck's OK.'

They continued the drive up the promontory toward Nutmeg Hill.

It was over an hour since the bomb had been placed in her car. There had not been an explosion. The detonation should have reverberated across the town and bounced between the hills that bordered the river. The sound should have echoed down the valley and the firehouse horn would have wailed its alarm in response. There would have been police, fire and ambulance sirens, and perhaps a plume of smoke curling over this small town located at the crook of the Connecticut River.

Why hadn't the bomb gone off? It had been carefully placed. It had been wired to the starter motor and should have exploded with the first turn of the ignition key.

Why had it not exploded?

Fourteen

Patrolman Jamie Martin was uncomfortable as he stood on the front stoop of Nutmeg Hill. His right hand held an acetate evidence bag containing a fluffy rabbit slipper with long floppy ears. He glanced from side to side as if expecting a last-minute reprieve, but the only welcome was a dawn light that streaked the Connecticut River and enticed tendrils of mist from the water's surface. After a final nervous shift he punched the bell.

'It's too damn early for this sort of thing,' he muttered aloud.

'That's for sure,' the disembodied voice of Lyon Wentworth said over the exterior intercom system. 'What do you want, Jamie?'

'The chief assigned the case to me, sir.'

The door clicked open to reveal Lyon standing in the entryway with bare feet below a bright yellow bathrobe.

'I see you've retrieved my wife's slipper. Come in and have some coffee.' Without waiting for an answer he padded his way through the house to the kitchen. He was astonished that Rocco would assign a sensitive matter such as the Morgan killing to a young patrolman like Martin.

Jamie obediently followed while nervously clearing his throat. 'Actually, this is official police business, Mr Wentworth.'

'Got something new on the Morgan case?' Lyon asked as they entered the kitchen. He poured two large mugs from the Mr Coffee machine on the counter. 'Cream and sugar?'

'Yes, sir, thank you. No, it isn't about the murders.' He carefully placed the bagged slipper on the counter before accepting a mug. He sipped the hot liquid a moment before he continued

147

in a rapid rush of words. 'If this slipper is identified as hers, I'm here to bust Senator Wentworth.'

'I didn't realize bad taste was illegal,' Lyon said over the rim of his coffee mug.

'What bad taste?' Bea said as she shuffled into the kitchen. Her hair was tousled and she wore a bulky terry-cloth robe and one animal slipper that was the mate to the one in the evidence bag. 'Hey, thanks for bringing in my other bunny. I must have dropped her on the terrace last night.' She flipped the acetate bag from the counter and tore it open before the horrified officer was able to secure the evidence. She stuffed her other foot into the rescued rabbit and poured coffee.

'I'm sorry those rabbits are yours, ma'am. I am obliged to point out that they are evidence in a crime.' The police officer fumbled in his shirt pocket for a small memo pad. 'Chief Herbert's instructions are,' he read slowly and precisely from the pad, '"Stake out the Camelot construction project." That's that thing next door.'

'We are familiar with the monstrosity,' Lyon said.

'Anyway, the chief said I was to bust the vandalizing perp bastards. Those were his exact words, sir. Who are defacing the property with their spray-paint graffiti. Last night I secreted myself on the premises as ordered. At approximately three hundred hours a person of unknown identity was observed with a circular object in her hand. She was painting the words "Through these portals pass . . ." in large letters on a wall.'

'How do you know it was a woman?' Lyon snapped.

Jamie Martin looked up from his monotone reading. 'In bunny slippers?'

'I resent the sexism inherent in that remark,' Bea said.

Jamie sighed and continued. 'I instituted apprehension movements after warning the suspect that I was a police officer. Unfortunately, during the ensuing pursuit I fell into a concrete form. The spray-paint perpetrator disappeared into the bordering woods. After changing into a fresh uniform I returned to the location. At that point in time I discovered an article of footwear next to the abandoned spray-paint can. Said footwear, in the shape of a rabbit, was tagged as evidence

148

and an interrogation was made at a nearby dwelling.' He looked up. 'That's as far as I've gotten so far.'

'I've heard of Cinderella, but this is ridiculous,' Lyon said with a sigh.

'I meant to wear my running sneaks,' Bea said, 'but I was sleepy.' Lyon stared at her in amazement. 'Well, don't look at me that way. Sometimes the democratic process breaks down and we are forced to take to the barricades in protest.'

'In this instance, that seems to mean taking to the construction site in our rabbit feet.'

'The charges are: vandalism, defacing private property, mischievous mischief, trespassing, and the chief says he will think of more charges later.'

'I think Rocco is pissed because of your criticism,' Lyon said to Bea.

'Can I come down to the station to turn myself in a little later this morning, Jamie?' Bea asked. 'I'd like to get showered and dressed first. Actually, being arrested works into my schedule this morning, since my car is parked in front of the police services building.'

'It was towed on the chief's orders,' Jamie said with a flush.

'Boy, Rocco really is pissed,' Lyon said as he poured everyone a second cup of coffee.

'You can obtain your vehicle by paying the fifty-dollar fine, along with storage and tow charges, at Proman's Salvage Yard,' Jamie Martin concluded.

Bea slammed her mug down with a thunk. 'That's it! Rocco's gone too far this time. He knows that Ralston Proman is a professional Korean War Veteran who's been bugging me on that memorial stuff for years. I'll be his captive audience for an hour when I go to reclaim my car.'

'I'd get it for you if I could. We'll see you later at the station, Jamie,' Lyon said as he ushered the officer to the door. When he returned to the kitchen, Bea was whipping eggs for omelettes. Lyon began to slice slivers of onions, ham and green pepper. 'I know you've been busy digging for information on the murders,' he said. 'Do you have anything yet?'

Bea added his cuttings to her omelette construction. 'On this one, I've had to call favors that don't even exist. God only knows what future price I'm going to have to pay for some of this information.'

'What did you turn up?'

She served plates while he buttered toast. 'Like Clay Dickensen is in deep financial difficulty and needed the cash money from that trust fund in the worst way.'

'I thought his accounting business was quite successful?'

'It is, but he's extremely overextended in his other interests. Did you know that condominium project where he lives was developed by CD Construction, which is completely owned by Clay? Evidently the job was underestimated and has soaked up money like a blotter. Slow sales have exacerbated the situation and the interest charges are eating him up. He's sixty days in arrears on his construction-loan payments to the bank. He's in so deep with some subcontractors that they are nearly ready to file mechanics' liens against the property. If liens are filed, construction loan advances will stop, and then the whole house of cards topples. At that point his position becomes untenable and it turns into foreclosure time. That action will affect his accounting firm, as most business accounts don't want to do business with a bankrupt CPA.'

'He's rescued if there's money in the trust fund?'

'Which there is. Despite what the twins thought, Morgan hadn't touched the trust's principle. It turned out that he had made a great deal of money on commodity futures. His broker's trade records verify this.'

'I haven't forgotten the fact that on the night of the Morgan murder Clay worked at my desk most of the evening. The combination to the RV door was jotted on paper taped to the desk pull-out. He might have seen it and guessed what it was. That gives Clay opportunity. Your information reveals that he certainly had a stronger motive than we thought.'

'Rina's not far behind her twin in the motive market,' Bea continued as she sat at the breakfast-nook table and attacked her omelette. 'Did you know that after she dropped out of college she followed the Grateful Dead rock group around the country? She was what they call a Dead Head?'

'Yes, I'd heard that from Clay.'

'And did you know that Morgan finally located her at one of the concerts, stoned out of her mind?'

'That's no big deal these days.'

'It was to Morgan,' Bea said. 'He played elaborate head games with her until she agreed to a commitment to the Institute of Living in Hartford.'

'A psychiatric hospitalization for smoking pot? That's rather extreme,' Lyon said.

'Morgan always operated on his own perceptions, never by ordinary values and social rules. Rina was kept there for nearly a year. She never forgave her older half-brother for that little sojourn.'

'After we found Skee's body, I left the room to make a phone call. When I returned, she had moved the barbell off his neck.'

'That lady is physically very strong.' Bea said.

'Were you able to find anything more about her murdered lover, Skee what's-his-name?'

Bea looked at crumpled notes she took from her robe pocket. 'There's not a great deal to find out about Skee Chickering. He was a physical-fitness drifter. He spent a lot of time working-out on muscle beaches in California. He entered a couple of body contests but never placed. He had a haphazard work history as a beach boy, a construction carpenter working off the books, and other casual pickup jobs.'

'Twins with motives and opportunity,' Lyon said. 'It would not be unusual for brother and sister to act in concert.'

'You think that Rina and Clay did it together?' Bea replied.

'Anything else?' Lyon asked.

'The documentation that Morgan had on Ernest and Garth is still missing. Whoever stole it from Morgan's office has either hidden or destroyed the papers. Speaking of destroying things, let's not forget that Garth is a killer trained through the courtesy of the US Army.'

'I know. He was an infantry leader and had Ranger training.

By definition that makes him expert in a lot of mayhem,' Lyon said. 'Except that, so far, no one has been blown up with C-4 or strangled to death with piano wire. Our present catalog of murder includes a sword, a long-range rifle shot, and a bizarre strangulation. That's a macabre pattern, but not military in nature.'

'It's no kind of pattern,' Bea said. 'You should consider Ernest now that you've mentioned a long-range rifle shot.'

Lyon scraped the remains of their meal into the garbage disposal and put the plates in the dishwasher. He leaned against the kitchen counter. 'When I landed the cloudhopper on the church, Ernest rushed out carrying his rifle. Rocco confiscated it for tests, but before that could be done it disappeared from the patrol car.'

'I don't know a thing about rifles,' Bea said, 'but those in Ernest's gun cases looked expensive.'

'I think there's a lot of money sunk in that collection.'

'If he stole the gun back from Rocco, would he destroy it, or would he clean it and put it back in the gun rack?'

'Let's find out,' Lyon said. He snicked the kitchen wall phone from its bracket and punched in a series of numbers. 'Good morning, Miss Harnell, is your brother there . . .? A sudden vacation. You don't know where.' He looked toward Bea with a raised eyebrow. 'He's either in Spain, France or Africa, but Ketchum, Idaho is in the running. Would it be possible for me to stop by the house today and look at some of Ernest's rifles . . .? They're all gone. All of them stolen? Thank you.' Lyon hung up. 'You caught the gist of that.'

'It's a convenient time to go on a secret vacation and have weapons stolen,' she said.

They moved in the practiced unison of a long-married couple as they cleared the table and straightened the kitchen.

'It's time to go after your car and be arrested. I do think they'll release you on your own recognizance.'

'Thanks a lot,' she said. 'I've arranged through the Attorney General's office for us to go through Morgan's RV, which is at the state police garage.'

'Captain Norbert must have loved that.'

'You can guess how ecstatic he was, but the forensics

people are done with it. We're allowed to prowl through if accompanied by a trooper escort. I promised we wouldn't remove or handle anything. Why don't we do that now and go for the car at noon? With a bit of luck my Korean War buddy might be at lunch. He's a big Legion supporter so noon is probably time to report to their bar.'

Lyon nodded. 'Good. I'd like another look at Morgan's armored vehicle. We still don't know how the killer got in.'

Like a glowering southern governor from decades past who stood in a schoolhouse door, Captain Norbert blocked the entrance to the state police garage. He stood arms akimbo and feet apart as he frowned at the Wentworths.

'I am against this,' he said. 'I admit you under protest on a direct order from my superior. Let the record so reflect.'

'Got it down, Captain,' the corporal with the steno pad said.

Norbert stepped aside at the last moment to let the Wentworths enter the building. He doggedly followed them. 'You are civilians in a restricted area. Any incorrect action on your part might break the chain of evidence.'

'We don't intend to run off with the RV,' Lyon said.

'We already know that Satan worshipper did it. So, why don't you two quit this sick rubbernecking?'

'I wonder when the next state police appropriation bill comes before my committee?' Bea whispered in a sotto voice loud enough to guarantee that both police officers heard.

The recreational vehicle stood alone in the dimly lit garage. A layer of dust had filtered through the front doors to cover it. Recessed overhead lights in wire baskets cast a dull glow directly over the vehicle, but left the side areas in shadows. The rear door was unlatched and open a few inches.

'Don't touch a damn thing,' Captain Norbert said.

'I thought the lab work had been completed?' Bea asked.

'It has, but I don't want some smartass defense attorney discovering that we let civilians search the murder scene. He'd be certain to create inanities to confuse some retard jury.'

Bea rolled her eyes at Lyon.

'Can I turn on the RV's interior lights?' Lyon asked.

'No,' Norbert answered. 'I'll do it.' He reached inside and threw a switch. 'The bodies are falling like ten pins in Murphysville and I have a politico checking on a stale murder scene.'

'Morgan's death is the first piece of the puzzle,' Lyon said. 'If we can find out how the killer got into the locked van, it might give us a lead to who he is. It would be a start toward finding our way out of the whole maze.'

'The killer's already in custody.'

Captain Norbert made Bea once again consider the political reality of fascism. The partial infrastructure for a full fascist dictatorship was already in place.

Lyon stepped inside the recreational vehicle. Blood-spattered walls attested to the furious carnage that had occurred here. During the mini-second that the heart continued beating, the blood spout must have been immense.

As he walked slowly down the center aisle, he noted that the vehicle was still an impregnable fortress. The armor plates that Morgan had lowered over the windows had not been removed. The front of the vehicle containing the driver's area was still untouched. The heavy windshield glass, similar to that used on armored trucks, was still secure. The doors in the driver's compartment had been welded shut.

There was only one entrance to the RV and that had been closed and securely locked on the night of the murder. And yet, someone had found a way to enter and kill Morgan. The murderer had left with the RV still locked.

Lyon was convinced that he was the only person who knew the combination of the door. Bea's intuitive guess pinpointed where his scribbled number reminder was kept, but no one else would have that knowledge. It seemed unlikely that Clay had accidentally discovered the numbers and immediately recognized the unlabeled symbols for what they were.

Did Morgan let someone in voluntarily?

On several occasions on the night of Morgan's murder, Lyon had seen various individuals attempt to get inside the

RV. Morgan had turned everyone away, including his lover from Boston.

'God, it's hot in here,' Bea said.

'The deceased put in one hell of a giant air conditioner because of the armor,' Norbert said. He pointed to the large unit's vent in the center of the ceiling. 'But you guys can swelter or leave, because we're not turning it on.'

Lyon ran his hands over the ceiling and around the air-conditioning vent. His fingers moved over the vent louvers. Bea watched his actions with interest and seemed to sense his thought process.

'Don't mess with things, OK?' Captain Norbert said.

'I believe this unit is merely set down into the roof and is not bolted to the frame,' Lyon said.

'We are not idiots here, Wentworth,' Norbert said. 'That fact was noted. We examined the roof from the outside and found no scratches or tool marks. We checked with the manufacturer. That unit would require at least four or five very strong guys to lift. If a tow truck or other such winch device were used to move the unit, it would cause drag marks across the roof. No way was that unit taken out of that ceiling without leaving some sort of marks on the roof.'

Lyon stopped his examination. 'In that case, there's no way to get in here except through the door.'

'None that I can see,' Bea responded. 'And yet we know the door was locked.'

'Will you two stop underestimating the professionalism of my command?'

'Your men weren't able to find any means of access, either through the frame or under the chassis?' Lyon asked the state police officer.

'No. There are no removable panels, traps, or anything of that nature. The deceased obviously knew the killer and admitted him of his own volition.'

'I thought you were convinced that Winston Crawford was the killer?' Lyon asked.

'He talked his way in then,' Captain Norbert said with a flush. 'Hell, who knows? Maybe Morgan was worried about the publicity damaging the university's reputation.'

'That night he didn't seem inclined to let anyone inside,' Lyon countered. 'Much less an anarchist sworn to kill him.'

'I don't believe in the tooth fairy or locked-room murders,' Norbert said. 'There's a simple explanation for the killer's means of entry. He came through the door. What could be more logical? And if I remember correctly, Wentworth, you had the combination to the door and were half swacked that night. You also ended up with the murder weapon. If Crawford didn't do it, we're back to square one. And guess who's numero uno on that square? You, Wentworth. Are we through in here now? I'm hot as hell.'

Bea Wentworth turned the pickup's air conditioner on high as they drove toward Proman's Salvage Yard on the Murphysville Turnpike. 'That didn't accomplish much,' she said. 'We're no further along than we were. Maybe Norbert is right. The anarchist did it.'

The van stopped at the curb a block from the police services building. The driver looked with astonishment at the four parking places directly in front of the building. A telephone repair truck and a red convertible occupied two of those spots. The other two were vacant. Senator Wentworth's compact car was not to be seen.

It was obvious that there had been no explosion here. The bomb had not gone off. But that was impossible. The material was of the finest quality and had been field tested in a remote Maine location. The detonation device was of simple design with more than adequate power from the car's own electrical system.

There was absolutely no way that bomb would not go off once that starter engine turned over. It had to blow, unless . . . and there was only one possible explanation – unless it had been discovered. The insertion of the device must have been observed by someone knowledgeable enough to realize what was happening. That risk was always a possibility, although quite remote.

If that were the case and the device was properly disarmed and recovered, bomb experts would be working on the origin of the parts at this very moment. Forensics laboratory people would lift fingerprints from the material.

No care had been taken to avoid prints on the explosive packages. Why bother to take such precautions when they were going to blow into a thousand fragments?

If they did not have names already, they might shortly.

The two people responsible must pay.

Lyon drove the pickup into Proman's Salvage Yard. He stopped in front of a peeling house trailer set on concrete blocks, which acted as the office. There was a surrealistic aura to the devastated automobiles that surrounded them in varying degrees of destruction. On the right were dozens of high stacks containing crushed machines, each barely two feet in width. On their left was a vast graveyard of wrecked automobiles that stretched for acres. Interspersed throughout the yard were piles of parts divided into hub caps, doors, hoses, and inexplicably, baby car seats.

Ralston Proman's greying hair was clipped in a short crew-cut. He wore an American Legion overseas hat and a silk-screened tee shirt which read 'Remember Korea'. He slouched over to the pickup's window and leaned on the sill. 'Give you fifty bucks for this heap and not a penny more. Only that generous cuz you were able to drive it in here.' His jaw drooped as he looked past Lyon. 'Senator Wentworth! I didn't expect to see you being driven around in a mess like this.'

Bea waved a greeting and beamed her best political smile. 'Good morning, Ralston. I was afraid I'd miss you because it's lunch hour.'

'They're painting the Legion today, Senator, otherwise I'd be belly up to the bar talking old war times with my buddies.'

'It would seem that they impounded my car, Ralston,' Bea said.

Proman stepped backward as if struck in the chest by a massive blow. 'Must be a mistake, Senator Wentworth. Why, if the guys down at the Legion knew that, we'd 'a put a human shield around your vehicle.'

'Thank you, Ralston,' Bea said with another ingratiating

smile, 'but I don't think human shields will be necessary today. Let me just pay the fee and drive away. I do have many errands,' she said hopefully.

'Hot damn!' Proman said. 'I shoulda' known. The vehicle with the Legislator marker plate. I'll get it for you, Senator. The keys were still in the ignition when they towed her in here. Be right back.' He sprinted around the corner of the office as fast as aging legs and incipient cirrhosis allowed.

'Why do I have a feeling that this state is going to gain a very large Korean War Memorial?' Bea said.

Lyon started to answer as a massive explosion spewed wreckage high in the air. They ducked as close to the engine firewall as they could huddle as metal began to fall in a hail of scrap around the battered pickup.

Fifteen

Bea Wentworth's legs were rigid as they shoved against the pickup's floorwell. Her fingers pressed against the dashboard, which pushed her shoulders deep into the seat cushions. She stared blankly ahead as small jaw muscles pulsated in an uneven rhythm.

Lyon leaned against the outside of the vehicle with his palms resting on the warm roof and his forehead pressed against the top rim of the window's safety glass.

Activity swelled in the salvage yard with the arrival of more vehicles. Sirens approached from two directions while the town's fire alarm blared in the distance.

The volunteer ambulance had been the last to arrive. Jamie Martin used chopping hand signals to direct two EMTs pushing a gurney toward Bea's demolished car.

Lyon waited for the inevitable.

It took five seconds before the first EMT, Bert Tandrum, Murphysville's corpulent Allstate Agent, scurried back around the edge of the office. He ran with bulging cheeks and both hands clamped tightly over his mouth. He barely made it behind the compressed car stack before he lost it.

With the exception of two police officers, those at the scene were volunteers. They were tradesmen from shops near the green, or second and third shift workers donating free time to the community. They were the firemen hosing down smoldering pieces of strewn wreckage. They were the auxiliary police constables directing traffic in front of the salvage yard, and they were the Emergency Medical Technicians.

The EMTs were trained for a crisis that included cardiac arrests, drownings, or car accidents. They had not expected to view the violent carnage the explosion had wreaked on Ralston Proman.

'Can we leave?' Bea asked. 'I don't know how much more of this I can take.'

'As soon as possible,' Lyon answered. 'I thought we should wait until Rocco arrives and we give him some sort of statement.'

'The bomb was meant for me,' Bea said. 'It was probably wired to the ignition. My car was towed in here, but it exploded the instant Proman started the engine. If I hadn't driven you home last night, I would have started the car then.'

There was no argument with her logic. Lyon had immediately perceived the significance of the sequence after the explosion. He had hoped her ignorance of bombs and detonators might keep her from putting it together.

Jamie Martin swaggered toward them.

'Oh, Lord,' Lyon mumbled. 'Don't let what I think is happening to this officer actually be happening.' He was seeing signs that unexpected authority had created its own monster.

'Yo, Wentworth,' Martin said. 'I want Senator Wentworth down at the station for her trespassing arrest. Posthaste. Now.'

'Somehow, Jamie, under the circumstances, that request pales into insignificance.'

The young officer flushed. 'Is the senator resisting arrest?'

'Later, Jamie,' Bea said tiredly. 'Tomorrow OK?'

'You did not seem to hear me,' the police officer responded in the distinctly separated words of a drill sergeant. 'Tomorrow is not satisfactory.'

'We are going home,' Lyon said as he slipped behind the wheel of the pickup and turned the ignition.

'Don't move that vehicle!' Jamie said as he stepped in front of the truck. His hand slid toward his holster.

'You touch that weapon and you will regret it for the rest of your life,' Lyon said. Their eyes locked. 'Where in the hell is Rocco?'

The police officer's fingers slid closer to the holstered revolver and then hesitated. 'He had to go into Hartford to federal court. We have an emergency call in for him.'

160

'Listen,' Lyon said in a gentle voice. 'You are in charge of this scene, Jamie. For God's sake forget the trespassing for today and look around you. You have a victim whose family must be notified. Have you called the ME?' Jamie looked blank. 'You have a bomb situation here that is far beyond your capabilities. Ask the state for scientific help. They have bomb experts. Cordon this area off. Run the department like Rocco would if he were here. Can you do that?'

'Yes.' Jamie hesitated another moment and then stepped aside. Lyon backed the pickup out of the salvage yard and began the drive to Nutmeg Hill.

The roiling hate that had been partially defused with the shedding of blood was beginning to rise again. Its focus was narrowly directed toward the meddling couple who had complicated all future plans.

The conclusion was simple. They must be destroyed. The original intention had been to kill the woman first. Through quirky luck they'd managed to overcome that threat, but at least the bomb had finally detonated. They were already suspicious, which put them on the alert and increased their investigative activities to the point where they might discover the truth.

The Wentworths must perish! The next attempt would be simple in execution. The final attack would utilize the most direct and surest way to eliminate them.

They would be dead before this day was out.

They did not speak during the ride back to the house. From time to time Lyon looked at his wife as she stared grimly ahead. Her features were taut as she sat stiffly erect.

'This killing has to stop,' she said in a voice barely audible over the wheezing thump of the pickup's laboring engine.

'I know,' Lyon replied.

'If we don't end it, it won't stop until we're dead.'

Lyon was silent. There was no easy answer. 'Since the legislature's not in session, why don't you go away for a few weeks?'

'Like where?' she asked without interest.

161

'I was thinking of that place in Maine we went to a few years ago. You remember, the cottage on Little Diamond Island in Casco Bay? You'd be isolated and safe, with an opportunity to recharge your batteries.'

She snapped him a sharp look. 'You know I can't do that and leave you alone.'

'I'm concerned about your safety. That bomb was planted in your car, not in my truck.'

'It was meant for both of us.' Her outburst seemed to have drained her. She shifted on the seat until she was turned toward him. 'I'm not going to live in terror. We'll go through this together.'

Lyon turned the pickup into the long drive that led up to the house. He unconsciously slowed as they neared the end of the promontory. Their home, perched on the highest point of the bluff, had darkened windows that bracketed the red front door in a manner that seemed to create a jack-o-lantern face. Once again the total effect had switched their home to a place of menace.

Bea's shiver told Lyon that the feeling of unease had been transmitted between them.

'Even our house has changed,' she said in a quiet voice.

He parked near the front door and quickly left the truck. He stood in the center of the drive and visually searched the lawns and tree lines in all directions. The driveway down to the highway was empty. The fields on either side of the house contained only a lone brown rabbit momentarily posture-frozen near the trees. The only movement was in the gentle wave of tall grass as a wind swept up from the river.

She stood by his side. 'What are you going to do now?'

'I'm going to search the house and barn to make sure we're secure,' he said. 'Later, we'll write a statement for the police, but before that I want to think through all that's happened. The best place to do that is up in the cloudhopper.'

She groaned. 'You have got to be kidding? We're practically under siege, and you're going to fly in the sky like a bobbing target in a shooting gallery.'

'I'll stay nearby and keep an eye on the roads and other approaches to the house.'

162

'I still think you're making a target of yourself. We'd be better off in a storm cellar.'

'We don't have a storm cellar,' Lyon replied.

'Maybe we both could go to Little Diamond Island?' He shook his head and she knew that further argument was useless. Lyon could be a very stubborn person. She suspected that he expected some sort of imminent attack, and this was his way of placing himself in jeopardy in order to protect her.

She followed as he walked briskly through the house, opening and shutting closet doors, looking into each room, and checking the security of window locks and doors. When he was convinced that no monsters lurked within their home, they searched the two outbuildings. They finished in the barn, where Lyon wheeled the balloon cart into the yard. He began to spread the envelope out on the grass preparatory to inflation.

Bea picked up the parachute harness, which was attached to a ring hung below the balloon's bottom aperture. She ran her fingers over the webbing and shook her head. 'If you're so intent on ballooning, why not fly in something substantial? At least you'd be in a real gondola and not dangling from a belt a thousand feet up. I'll help you launch the Wobbly II, if you want?'

'No, thanks. I can get the cloudhopper in the air fast and get down quickly if need be.'

They worked as a well-trained team as they unrolled the envelope and arranged it for inflation. Lyon started the small compressor that blew air into the balloon until it was filled sufficiently for the interior to be heated. When the bag began to billow, he braced the propane burner across his waist. He directed the nozzle through the aperture, adjusted the propane gas flow, and lit it. The flame jet quickly heated the interior air. Slowly the balloon began to rise. It bobbed from side to side as hot air increased its buoyancy. When the bag was erect, he hooked the propane burner to the ring and tied a line to the metal mooring post anchored in cement by the barn.

Bea shook her head as he slipped into the parachute harness.

'I'm not usually an overly anxious person,' she said. 'I've flown with you more than a hundred times in the Wobbly I and II, but this damn cloudhopper is scary.'

'Ho ho ho!' Lyon said as he adjusted the propane burner. He lit another burn for adjustment until the balloon bobbed at the end of its tether. 'If I stay away from high-tension lines, and watch where I come down . . .'

'Like on church steeples?'

'I miscalculated.'

'You know, most sane people who want to ruminate sit on the porch and slowly rock back and forth.'

'I find ballooning very conducive for abstract thought of a nonlinear nature.'

'Your nonlinear mind may be vertically challenged when that toy decides to make a rapid descent. I hate it so much that I am tempted to sneak out here some night and slice it to ribbons.'

He stopped his preflight check to smile. 'The midnight rectifier strikes again. Give her a can of spray paint or scissors and she'll convince you of anything.'

'Believe in me,' she said. 'The New England genes that made my ancestors spice Boston Harbor with tea are still active.'

'I want you to take your New England genes inside and stay away from windows and doors,' Lyon said. 'Better yet, go to the rec room and bolt the door.'

'You mean, get out of the line of fire,' Bea said, 'while you drift over half the state making a target larger than Humpty Dumpty.'

'The wind is from the sea. I'll be safely over the river and won't be a target.' He released the mooring line. Another short burst of flame from the burner changed the balloon's lift. It quickly rose two hundred feet while he dangled from the harness. 'Go inside!' he yelled down at Bea.

She shook her head and began to walk toward the tool shed.

The cloudhopper's ascent to 1,000 feet was rapid due to the excess buoyancy. At that height the balloon leveled off and Lyon gave only occasional propane burns in short quick bursts to maintain equilibrium. He grasped the harness lines overhead to stabilize his body swing before he looked down.

Bea hadn't returned to the house as he had requested. She had taken a hoe from the tool shed and was working in the small vegetable garden planted on the sunny side of the barn. He should have suspected that she'd react that way. As frightened as she was, and he knew how deeply the exploding car had affected her, she would refuse to withdraw and cower. It was not in her nature to cringe at every creak and shift of their ancient house. She would not allow herself to believe that normal noises were a prelude to some marauder's attack. She might be frightened, but she would not surrender to a paralysis of fear.

A thousand feet above the surface of the river gave him a commanding view of the surrounding road network. No cars were traveling toward Nutmeg Hill. Except for a single van parked near the crane, the workers had left the construction site for the day. If there was a stalker, he either hadn't started yet or was working his way toward them through a mile of woods.

A five-mile-an-hour sea breeze carried the balloon northwest and parallel to the meandering course of the Connecticut River. He could see Clay's condominium development with its new construction on the north side of the artificial lake.

The sniper who killed Bambi had fired from the second house. It had been a long shot across the water into the top of the Boston woman's head. It was a difficult shot, but not an impossible one if the rifle were supported on the window ledge and the victim motionless.

The murder of the topless dancer was worrisome. Why bother? What threat did she pose to anyone? Her only interest was in the financial protection of her son. That was hardly threatening to anyone, and only a minor inconvenience to Morgan. Lyon doubted that she was involved in any murder conspiracy, and that would be the only valid reason to eliminate her. Then why bother to kill her? Unless she was not the intended victim.

He examined the condominium again and drew an imaginary line from the shooter's position to the chaise lounge.

165

There was a possibility that the killer did not know who was occupying the lounge. The ordinary assumption anyone would make was that Clay was the one on the deck. Unless the killer actually saw who came out to the lounge, distance and the angle of the body would make definite identification impossible.

The wind began to shift as eddies from the north changed the balloon's drift. Lyon gave the burner lever a few tugs to maintain altitude.

The balloon gradually reversed direction and began to drift toward the sea. The new course would carry it back over Nutmeg Hill.

If errors had been made in Bambi's murder, perhaps there were other inconsistencies that had been overlooked. He thought back over the details of Morgan's death.

His sherry and Morgan's Pernod meant that he and the dead man shared a common desire for slightly unusual drinks. It was entirely possible that they had both been given a slow-acting drug. Lyon was convinced that he had suffered from some type of hallucinogen that completely confused him when he was chased through the woods. Morgan might have suffered from another sort of narcotic whose effect kept him from hearing anyone attempting to enter his RV.

Anyone at the house that night could have contaminated the liquor. The bottles on the bar cart were accessible to everyone throughout the evening.

The wind had carried him back over Nutmeg Hill. The balloon's shadow fell across Bea as she worked in the garden. She looked up and waved.

The most important clue to the puzzle lay on the ground before him.

As the balloon's huge shadow slowly crept across the lawn, Lyon realized that the answer could only be revealed from this particular angle and height.

He was now able to see the nearly imperceptible tracks that crossed the grounds of Nutmeg Hill. The shallow ruts across the meadow and lawn stopped at a point only a short distance from the drive where Morgan's van had been parked.

Backtracking, the faint indentations led across the meadow

to a cut in the tree line that entered the construction site. The tracked crane that had created the ruts was parked at the corner of the partially completed building.

The killers knew that Morgan and Lyon were drugged. They had driven the crane to the edge of Nutmeg Hill's drive. The cable had been lowered and attached to the air-conditioning unit in the center of the RV's roof. The crane had lifted the unit straight up a distance of less than two feet, not far enough to rip the wiring loose. The unit's temporary extraction opened a hole large enough for someone to slip into the vehicle, murder the drugged Morgan, and leave without a trace. The crane had then carefully replaced the air conditioner in its slot without leaving a mark on the roof of the RV. With everything in order the crane had retreated across the yard back into the construction site.

Lyon knew who had killed Morgan and the others.

The slow drift of the balloon had carried it past Nutmeg Hill toward the apartment-building construction.

He looked down and saw the killer framed in the window of the crane. The cab window had been lowered so she could lean out with support as she carefully aimed the rifle.

It was immediately apparent that Bea was the intended target. She was innocently working in the garden and would be an extremely easy target for anyone with the slightest ability with a rifle. Lyon knew full well that Rina's marksmanship was far from rudimentary.

'Rina!' He yelled as loud as he could. 'Dead Head, look up here!'

For the briefest of moments they were suspended in a wide tableau. Bea looked toward the crane in astonishment as she saw Lyon hovering above the construction site in the cloud-hopper's harness. Rina, five stories high in the crane cab, swivelled the rifle away from Bea to aim at the large over-head target.

Rina fired and immediately fired again.

Lyon saw that her shots were on target, but they were passing harmlessly through the balloon's envelope. Rina would quickly realize that the hits created holes too small for the loss of hot air to have any appreciable effect. He would be in trouble when she directed her fire toward him as he hung helplessly suspended in the harness.

Lyon pressed his legs together and began to pump back and forth as if swinging at a playground. His body began to swoop forward. He complicated the maneuver by violently lunging from side to side. His movements which had begun as a pendulum swing shifted into a skewered parabolic curve.

Rina fired a third time, but the bullet passed harmlessly to the side.

As the balloon began to drift past the crane, Lyon opened the full ripping panel for partial deflation. The balloon immediately dipped to an angle of descent that would carry it back to the yard at Nutmeg Hill.

This abrupt shift placed him in Rina's blind spot directly over the roof of the crane cab. Until he passed beyond the crane it would be impossible for her to get another shot at him. In the two heartbeats it took to pass over the crane, Lyon saw Bea still standing in the garden looking toward them. He knew Rina was probably stuffing more cartridges into the rifle's magazine.

The killer could shoot Bea at a time of her choosing. In another instant he would pass over the crane cab's roof on his downward trajectory. He would be only a few feet away and descending in a direct line away from Rina. Her aim would not have to lead him, and his wild body gyrations would not appreciably increase the complexity of the shot. She would probably be able to pump three bullets into him before he reached the ground.

With him dead or dying in the harness, Rina could leisurely target Bea as she stood in the center of the garden far removed from any ground cover. His wife would never survive a dash to the protection of the house.

Lyon's right foot scraped along the top edge of the crane cab. He brought his left foot back as the balloon drifted past the crane. As soon as he was clear he kicked out with all his strength. His instep caught under the forward stock of Rina's rifle and flipped it out of her hands. The weapon spun end over end as it looped over the rim of the promontory and fell toward the river.

168

The balloon's final descent was swift. Lyon hit the ground hard. He was able to stay on his feet by running with the partially deflated balloon as it bounced unevenly across the yard.

Bea grabbed him around the waist as he passed through the garden. She was pulled along with him as they plowed down a row of staked beefeater tomato plants. Lyon grabbed the mooring stanchion as they passed by the barn and they were able to tether the balloon.

Lyon simultaneously hit the harness quick release and pivoted to run at full speed back toward the construction site.

He glanced up at the tower crane. From his location directly underneath the jib, he could see that Rina was not on the superstructure, but she could be inside the cab. He began to climb the struts of the crane's climbing frame. He knew that as long as he was on the crane he was in a very vulnerable position. Although her rifle was gone, it was possible that Rina had a handgun.

He stopped to rest at the third story. There was still no sign of Rina, but she might be waiting until he reached the tower and approached the cab before she shot him in the face at point-blank range.

Stopping was a mistake. It allowed time for mental pictures to focus on frightening possibilities. He might reach the top only to stare into the barrel of her pistol. He would see the flash of the exploding shell for a microsecond, but would never hear its retort as the projectile pierced his brain and he fell from the crane. The image of his own death was vivid and real.

The others did not deserve to die. The last victim's sin was a badgering request for a memorial to valiant men.

Lyon closed his eyes tightly for a moment and then forced them open. He looked up and continued his climb.

He assumed that Bea would see what was happening and call 911 for help. He somehow felt that it was imperative to reach Rina before anything else happened.

He called to her as he neared the end of the climb. 'Rina! It's Lyon. I'm coming up.' No answer. So much for a dialogue.

169

He stopped again. Rina's ominous silence meant precautions were in order. He looked up and thought he might be able to work his way along the underside of the jib beneath the cab. If he reached a point behind the cab, he could swing up on the rear part of the jib at the counterweight. That position would place him out of sight and to the rear of the cab door. A strategic position might grant him at least a small element of surprise.

A climb of three more feet and he was able to reach up to a cross-strut underneath the jib. He let go of the climbing frame and hung from the jib. He swung his body forward and shifted one hand then the other to the next strut. He repeated the movement until he was behind the cab. He pulled up on the outside of the jib and swung his feet up over the edge to the side of the counterweight. Once secure, he was able to lever up the rest of his body.

If she came out of the cab to face him, she could still fire at close range. He moved quickly forward.

'Rina, you there?' he called as he yanked open the cab door and lunged for her.

It was empty.

Lyon stumbled into the cab and plunked down in its operator's seat. He began to tremble from exertion as the rush of adrenalin quickly receded with the removal of immediate danger. His breath came in short gasps as he fought to regain physical and mental control.

The crane was moving!

The lumbering metal behemoth slowly inched across the ground toward the edge of the promontory.

It would reach the rim of the cliff above the river in two dozen yards. Once the huge weight of the crane neared the promontory's lip it would tilt forward until the whole machine toppled into the river.

It was now apparent to Lyon that while he fought to land the balloon, Rina had left the top cab and gone down the ladder on the opposite side of the climbing frame. When she reached ground level she had hidden inside the crane's truck cab. Once she knew he had climbed too high for retreat, she had started the short drive to the cliff.

Lyon stood on the jib at the cab's door. It was too high to jump. Once the crane went over the cliff he doubted that anyone could survive the fall. He stepped further out on the narrow platform and clutched one of the cantilever cables. The crane was now only a few yards from the edge of the cliff. Far beneath him he saw Rina's head protrude from the lower cab door. She looked up at him with what he knew was a grimace of hate.

Rina used both hands to grasp the top edge of the cab in preparation for swinging the rest of her body out. The machine's forward momentum was slow enough to give her ample time to leave the driver's cab and make the easy jump to the ground. She had probably wedged the accelerator open to keep the monster machine on its path to destruction.

When the crane's leading edge reached the cliff, Rina still hadn't emerged any further from the cab. She looked up at him again. Her look of hate had turned to one of utter terror.

She screamed. It was a primeval cry of anguish and death.

As he watched her writhe, Lyon realized that she was unable to leave the cab. For some unknown reason her lower body was trapped in the slowly moving vehicle. They would make the fatal plunge together.

The forward tracks of the crane's heavy body topped the cliff edge. The large vehicle seemed to hesitate a moment before it slowly tilted. When its center of gravity shifted, it began to fall.

Sixteen

'Wentworth!'

Bea hung in the cloudhopper harness a few feet to the side of the falling crane.

Lyon flung himself at her as the crane plunged toward the river. His hands closed over her right ankle like the awkward catch of a mediocre trapeze artist.

Bea was sufficiently aware of the cloudhopper's aerodynamics to know that the sudden addition of Lyon's weight would upset their equilibrium. A pronounced dip could entangle them in the crane's superstructure and force them to follow the falling machine down the cliff to destruction in the river. She immediately compensated for this by starting a long propane burn the instant he jumped.

Lyon's weight had caused the cloudhopper to sink a few feet before the added buoyancy of the burn took effect. They hovered motionless for a moment before the balloon began to slowly rise.

The fading Doppler sound of Rina's final scream followed their rise as the balloon's flight path made a parabolic sweep over the cliff above the river.

Lyon wrapped both arms around Bea's feet.

'This is not my idea of fun,' she said.

'Next week wicker gondolas only,' Lyon said as he shifted his grip. They faced in opposite directions. Bea's ability to see forward and control of the propane burner left her in command of the craft. 'Put us down as soon as we're over land,' he said.

'I think we have another problem. I'm seeing big round things.'

'Black specks before your eyes? You're going to lose consciousness?'

'I mean red and yellow beach balls,' she replied. 'I see a string of them in front of us.'

Lyon knew instantly that his wife was not having vision problems. The beach-ball objects were wire warnings that signaled high-tension lines to low-flying aircraft. The wire that crossed at this point originated at the atomic power plant near Haddam Neck and carried thousands of volts to the massive pylons that supplied power to the Hartford grid.

'A burn!' Lyon yelled. 'Give the propane a shot to get over the power line!' High-tension wires were the most feared obstacle for a hot-air balloonist. The huge craft's vertical-only control made them vulnerable to wire entanglements. Such collisions caused most of the sport's fatalities. 'For God's sake, give it a long burn!' he yelled.

'I am!' Bea yelled back. She was aware of their danger now that they were close enough for her to see the electrical wire supporting the colorful round markers. She yanked the burner lanyard again and again. The only response was a small sputter. 'There's no more propane,' she said.

'Pull the ripping panel! We may drop below it.'

It didn't take an expert balloonist to see that their present trajectory would not carry them under the power line. The ripping panel did not spill hot air quickly enough for the high balloon bag to clear the wire. 'We're going to hit it,' she said matter-of-factly.

Lyon looked down. If he made the long fall into the river from this point, his chances of survival were minimal. Since Bea had to pull up on the parachute harness in order to release enough tension to allow the quick release to operate, she would not be able to drop free fast enough. She had no survival odds. 'I'm staying,' he said.

'No,' she replied. 'Jump!'

'I like the view,' he said as he tightened his grip on her feet in anticipation of what he knew was going to happen next.

Bea attempted to kick him free. When his grip prevented that, she tried to scissor her legs in order to break his hold. 'Please, go. Lyon, please.'

'Nope.' He turned as far as he could to look over his

shoulder at the approaching wires. Her estimate was correct. Although their descent had begun, the balloon envelope would hit the wire before they had dropped far enough. Once contact was made, they would be electrocuted. 'I love you!'

'Me too!' she yelled back as her harness struck the wires.

The balloon envelope draped forward and began to deflate.

Lyon involuntarily grimaced in anticipation of the paralyzing shock that would momentarily course through their bodies.

'Doesn't electricity travel at the speed of light or something?' Bea asked.

'Something like that,' Lyon answered. He noticed that they had struck the wires near the southerly side of the river bank beyond the last of the beach-ball markers. From their point of impact the wire sloped toward the lower pylons on the far shore. As the balloon deflated, the bag began to slide slowly down the wire.

'What's happening?' Bea asked in a voice partially afraid to articulate the question for fear of invoking a worse calamity.

'For some reason the power's off,' Lyon said. 'We're sliding along the wire's slope. If we keep going, we can make the drop.'

The balloon envelope continued to creep down the wire. Lyon added the swing of his body to help speed its momentum. Although his hands were clamped tightly together around Bea's feet, their leaden feeling indicated that he would soon lose his grip. He only had seconds before the last of his strength ebbed and he fell.

They were still high above the river, perhaps too high. 'When I let go, pull up on the harness and snap the quick release.'

'You've got to be kidding! We'll drown.'

He didn't have time to reply. The last of the strength left his arms and he lost his grip. He dropped away from her. He attempted to keep his body straight during the fall in order to hit the water in an upright position.

He struck the river in a standing position and rapidly sank below the surface. The long descent seemed interminable and his awkward arm motions were useless. His strength was

174

gone and his arms felt like lead weights. His descent stopped as he gently touched a soft bottom. Lyon scissored his feet frantically through silt before he began to slowly rise. Could he hold his breath long enough to reach the surface? He tried an awkward swimming motion, but the slow jerky movements didn't help his ascent. The fall and fatigue had disoriented him. He had no comprehension of how long he had sunk or how deep under the water he was. He only knew that he wanted to breathe so desperately that in seconds he would involuntarily gasp for air.

A corner of his remaining conscious thought knew that if they were near the shore at the time of the drop, the river might not be too deep at this point.

He unexpectedly broke the surface. His head tilted up to gasp huge gulps of air before he flopped backwards and nearly sank again. He continued gasping for air, but found that he could remain on the surface by treading water.

Bea was upside down high above his head as she struggled with the harness of the deflated balloon. She had pulled her body up and was frantically punching the quick release. It finally worked! She dropped away from the remnants of the balloon and plummeted toward the river. She fell in a horizontal position with both arms and feet flailing.

As she hit the river, a wide plume of water sprayed up on either side as she sank below the surface.

He tried to swim toward the spot where she had disappeared under the water, but the tremors in his arms made his movements a pathetic dog paddle.

A boat pulled alongside. It was a long flat-bottom rowboat with a fisherman operator whose wide gnarled hands reached for him. He was halfway over the gunnels before he managed to flip into the bottom of the boat. 'My wife . . .' he choked.

'Ye-ap,' the oarsman said. 'Saw her fall.' He sat at the oars and dipped them deep into the water and pulled back in an easy fluid motion that spurted the boat ahead.

In another two minutes Bea was in the boat by Lyon's side gasping for breath.

'You two shouldn't play around those electric wires,' the fisherman said. 'If the power plant hadn't been closed down for refitting, youda' been fried.' He considered that thought a moment before he said, 'Striped bass is running.'

Some things are truly important, Lyon thought. And today striped bass was certainly one of them.

Lyon stood behind the computer monitor in his study and looked down at Nutmeg Hill's patio. The scene reinforced his conviction that there was a certain balanced symmetry in life.

The patio was festooned with Japanese lanterns which cast a warm amber glow across the deepening twilight. Rocco stood behind the large barbecue wearing an incongruously tall chef's hat and long butcher's apron. He spread glowing coals into a neat cooking pattern with a long-handled fork. His free hand clenched a tall drink in a translucent glass with a sprig of mint sprouting over the lip. He sipped on the drink as he continued his obsessive coal arrangements.

Martha Herbert stood by her husband's side holding a large tray of New York cut steaks. She smiled tentatively at the others on the patio.

Clay Dickensen stood alone at the far end of the parapet with one foot up on the stone wall. He was bent forward as if poised for a flight that would soon join the night and the river. His troubled look appeared to be a stare into the past in the hopes of learning a different outcome. This was his time to grieve, Lyon thought. It was a necessary time for him to come to terms with the pain the dissolution of his family had created. He was still young enough to find the strength that would allow him to survive. Time would be his succor and he would eventually heal.

Car headlights briefly swept across the patio and then blinked out as a new arrival parked in the driveway. Ernest Harnell, wearing a cream white suit and an outback hat worn at a rakish angle, limped up the patio steps. He paused dramatically and leaned on his blackthorn tree shillelagh.

The writer look-alike had arrived with at least several conversational gambits. Lyon considered the options to explain Ernest's injury: the bulls might have been exceedingly mean at Pamplona this year, or possibly there was a small plane crash near Victoria

176

Falls. Fighting in some distant civil war was always a possibility. He disregarded the latter. He knew the look of a man recently gored by a frenzied bull. It was probable that the answer would be elicited by Garth Wilkins as he forced his adversary through a sarcastic minefield.

Garth sat casually on the parapet, engrossed in conversation with Leslie. His attention shifted when he sensed the group's attention drawn toward Ernest. He made a studied slow turn to watch his fellow teacher limp across the patio. The sight of his rival's appearance forced Garth to change his posture and body language as if he were an ancient warrior girding for battle. Lyon had always considered Garth's attack-Ernest metamorphosis as something between a fighting ship of the line trimming for the attack, and a perched buzzard observing a parade of carrion while it selected tonight's meal.

Bea moved from group to group with an assorted tray of canapés and three types of greetings. The first smile was reserved for old friends like Rocco and Martha or Garth and Ernest. The second was her refined political 'gleam' which was flashed at her stalwart political supporters as represented by the rather loud group occupying the center of the patio. The third breed of smile was a small glimmer of resignation and understanding that from time to time she gave Lyon.

The world had been shaken, moved, and then returned to its ordinary orbit. As a result, it seemed as if nothing had changed.

Lyon knew that it was time to go to the patio and moderate a truce between the two college professors. If it wasn't done shortly, Ernest might be goaded into the use of his shillelagh for something other than walking. The dean of Middleburg University had once again requested Lyon's intervention. The college administration felt that the crisis in the English department had reached a critical juncture that needed immediate solution. The major problem was the impasse between the two men now girding for conflict on the patio.

Rocco flicked two completed steaks on a platter his wife held as Lyon came out on the patio. He glanced over at his friend and tilted his glass in salute as Martha served the meat to a group at the picnic table in the side yard.

'Norbie called as I arrived home,' Rocco said. 'He told me that this afternoon the state police divers finally got Rina's body out of the cab. The crane tilted over as it fell from the cliff. That, combined with the twisted metal, meant that she was buried deep in river-bottom silt. They had a hell of a time working underwater in all that, and had to dismantle the thing piece by piece until they reached her.'

'Could they tell why she never jumped out?'

Rocco nodded as he flipped more steaks on the coals. 'You bet. Simple enough thing. The bottom leg of her jeans had slipped over a gear lever on the floorboards. If she'd had another few seconds or didn't panic she would have either ripped loose or pulled it off.'

'What's the word on our hand-grenade-throwing friend Winston?' Lyon asked.

'The murder charges against him have been dropped, but he'll face charges on weapons possession and the rest of it. I think that's the end of the pathetic little band of college dropouts who call themselves the Brotherhood of Beelzebub.'

'Norbert and the state's attorney are completely satisfied it was Rina?' Lyon asked.

'Absolutely. They found incriminating clothing with blood specks hidden in the crawl space at the Exercise Place. The forensics lab thinks that the shot that killed Bambi may have been meant for Clay.'

'I'm not surprised at that,' Lyon said as he remembered his balloon flight over Clay's condo and his thought that the shooter may have made a mistake in identity. 'Rina wanted the whole pie for herself after she killed Morgan.'

'Right. Her lover, Skee, did have experience as an operating assistant on a crane, and he was capable of driving the thing. Rina was the one who went into the RV and dispatched Morgan. A real nice lady.'

'Bambi was killed in place of Clay, and Skee because he might talk?'

'That's the way everyone sees it.'

'Why was she after Bea?'

'Mixed feelings. She was afraid of what you two might find out, she wanted Nutmeg Hill, either with or without you, and I think the lady just went completely out to lunch.'

Lyon nodded and slipped away from the barbecue group and sat at the glass-topped table in the corner. He caught Garth's eye and gestured for him to join him. He gave a similar signal to Ernest. Both men warily pulled out wrought-iron chairs and sat at opposite ends of the table. Lyon's position between them immediately cast him as an unofficial moderator.

Garth smiled wickedly. 'OK, Papa, you've kept it to yourself long enough. How many guesses do I get about your limp? Gored by a bull? An old war wound . . .?'

'I tripped in a hotel shower in Atlantic City,' Ernest said.

'By the way, Ernest,' Lyon said. 'Did you ever get your stolen gun collection back?'

Ernest blushed. 'My sister had them,' the professor replied. 'She said I get them back after the Garden Club tour. She's got flower arrangements in my gun racks.'

'Naturally you're going to prosecute her,' Garth said.

'Enough, gentlemen,' Lyon said in a firm voice low enough to be distinctly heard by both men, but confidential enough to not travel beyond the table. 'The dean has asked me to talk with both of you.'

'Last time you tried to mediate for the department, people started to die,' Ernest said.

Lyon ignored the remark. 'The university has been placed in an untenable position concerning any decisions they make concerning your department,' Lyon said. 'You are both tenured teachers with extensive publications and excellent credentials in your fields.'

'And some of us have carried homophobia to new heights,' Garth said.

'I understand the army revoked your jump wings since you don't need a parachute to flit,' Ernest replied.

Lyon shook his head. 'That's it. This nonsense stops now. Do you both understand that?'

'I will not serve under this man as department head,' Garth said.

'For once we agree,' Ernest said.

'Your alternatives are as follows,' Lyon said. 'Either one

of you takes the department chair while the other assumes the endowed position, or both of those slots will be filled by outside people. It comes down to the fact that you either both stay and cooperate with each other or you both leave. You have five seconds to make your choice.' Lyon would have looked at a wristwatch to verify the sweep of the second hand if he had worn a watch. He mentally counted to five twice. 'Well?'

'How do I know he'll lay off me?' Garth asked. 'And how can they get rid of us with our tenure?'

'Because I have the documentation that Morgan collected,' Lyon said. 'If either of you persists, I will release Morgan's file. The resulting embarrassment will require resignations.'

Ernest looked at him in amazement. 'You've got that stuff?'

'Of course. Who did you think stole it?'

Both men looked at him with acceptance. Lyon realized, to his chagrin, that they considered him perfectly capable of breaking into Morgan's office and stealing whatever documents he wished. Although the men seated on either side appeared to be looking directly at him, they were actually observing each other. Their thoughts were undoubtedly similar. Each weighed the problems of changing positions. They had to consider the difficulty in obtaining tenure at an acceptable university. They had to also consider general teaching conditions, department politics, and all the complexities involved in changing the direction of their lives.

Ernest had deep roots in Murphysville. The home he occupied with his sister had been in the family for four generations. Its sale would be an emotional loss. Garth's home was new, but his attachment was also significant due to its unusual nature and the care they had taken in its creation. Its sale would also be a large loss if he were forced to relocate.

'Who gets which job if we stay?' Ernest asked.

The first step had been taken. That remark indicated a possible bridge. 'I've given it a great deal of thought,' Lyon replied as he laid a silver dollar on the table.

Garth laughed. 'But of course. We flip.' He thought a moment. 'What the hell. Do it.'

Lyon flipped the coin high in the air and caught it. He

slapped it on his wrist with his fingers covering the face. 'Ernest calls.'

Garth nodded. 'Why not.'

'No need,' Ernest said. 'I think I should take the Ashley and Garth the department chair. He's best suited for handling administrative details and dealing with people. I get impatient with that kind of stuff.'

Garth nodded and held out his hand to the other teacher. 'Agreed?'

'Agreed.'

They shook hands.

Lyon left the table with the two teachers involved in cooperative conversation for the first time in years. Leslie put a hand on his shoulder.

'You don't have the Morgan papers,' Leslie whispered to him. 'I took them.'

'Does Garth know that?'

'No. I didn't want him to think I was a common thief, even if I did steal them for his protection. I don't want them. Let me mail them to you in what they call the plain brown envelope. You know, I think it might work between those two.'

'I hope so,' Lyon said.

'There you are, Leslie,' Bea said as she took his arm. She gave Lyon an eyebrow signal toward Clay, who was standing alone at the parapet. 'Let me turn on the lawn floods and show you my garden. I'm considering putting in some new annuals and need your expert advice.' She led him away as Lyon moved toward the grief-stricken man in the shadows.

'Freshen your drink?' Lyon asked.

'No, thank you. I really shouldn't have come tonight. I'm sorry I'm such a morose guest.'

'No one expects you to be dancing jigs, Clay. You've had some shattering events in your life.'

'Did you always know it was Rina?'

'I first became suspicious when we discovered Skee's body. The gym door was locked from the outside, but rather than say Skee was probably out on an errand, she insisted on unlocking the door. It was as if she knew he was inside and wanted the body quickly discovered and removed. The final clue was revealed from the balloon when I saw the tracks across the side yard near the drive. It seemed apparent that the crane had been used to lift the RV's air-conditioner unit to gain entry into Morgan's Trojan horse. A climbing crane is a difficult machine to operate, but Skee Chickering had worked construction occasionally and very possibly had been exposed to crane operation.'

Clay nodded. 'I'd known for years that Rina hated Morgan with a passion. It wasn't just the money. She never forgave him for her forced commitment to the mental hospital. Even with that, it never occurred to me that she would turn to murder. I suppose the situation became critical when her emotions were matched with a strong need to get her hands on the trust fund principle. I abetted that situation since I was as desperate for the money as she was. It was evidently more than she could handle without violence.'

'And she was able to involve Skee in the scheme.'

'Hell, that beach boy used to sleep with anyone for a ten-dollar gratuity. He probably felt that getting their hands on the trust fund was the mother lode of all tips. Add that to the fact that my sister controlled the musclebound sociopath like a marionette, and you have a built-in accomplice. He was her buddy until something poisoned them.'

'We'll never really know what actually caused the break between them,' Lyon said. 'It's possible he was willing to go along with Morgan's for-profit murder but not the others. If not that, perhaps he tried to play a little game of extortion. Either alternative would guarantee his death warrant as far as Rina was concerned.'

'But why did she kill Bambi? That woman never harmed anyone, unless you consider topless dancing a mortal sin. Rina hardly knew her, and the fact that she was Morgan's lover didn't justify her murder.'

'Bambi was here to get money for the child she had with Morgan,' Lyon said. He did not add the possibility that Bambi had been killed accidentally by a shot Rina meant to kill her twin. With Clay dead the whole trust fund devolved to her. Bambi's accidental killing was knowledge

182

best kept from Clay. He had enough emotional baggage to carry.

'The insane greed of it!' Clay said. 'When we were young I was always the neat, quiet, calculating one, while Rina did everything in life with a vengeance. When she rode horses as a teenager, she had to jump the highest. When she became a rock groupie, she had to be the creepiest. When she decided to save an endangered species, it had to be the most majestic. Everything in her life was excessive.'

'It was a zest that could have been beneficial,' Lyon said. Unspoken between them was the bloodlust for killing that had somehow been unleashed during her first murder. Killing Morgan might have been greed, but during the commission of the act something evil within her had been released. There was no need to mutilate his body in that manner, just as there had been no need to kill Bambi or Skee in such a painful manner. Proman had been exploded, and Lyon and Bea were slated for her bullets in what had ultimately turned into a bloodlust. It would never have ended.

'God only knows, the money has been useful to me at this point in my life, but now there's more than I need,' Clay said. 'There's more than either of us would have needed.' He turned from his distant gaze into the night to look directly at Lyon. 'Bambi wanted a quarter of a million for her kid, so I've set up a trust for little Barney. And Rina's memorial is over there.' He pointed toward the condominium's naked steelwork.

'What?' Lyon asked in surprise.

'The developers of Camelot weren't too happy with their project. Due to the rocky location, costs were already out of hand. The units increased in price at a time when the condo market was soft. And that wasn't helped by Rina's unpleasant publicity. I gave them a fair price, if that's ever possible in a distressed project.'

'You bought the damn thing?' Lyon asked in astonishment.

'Yes. I'll have the high steel dismantled for salvage and the concrete that's already poured will be broken up and carted off. We'll bulldoze it down and reforest over what they've done so far. When the land is reclaimed, it will be donated to the land trust in perpetuity as the Rina Dickensen Bird Sanctuary. It's the best beginning I can make of her very bad ending.'

'It would be a natural habitat for eagles,' Lyon said.

'At this point, it's the only thing I can do for her and also attempt to make amends to you and Bea,' Clay said. He waved a hand over the patio. 'Rina wanted Nutmeg Hill in the worst way, you know? She knew you and Bea together would never sell it. I'm sure it occurred to her that with Bea gone she'd have a couple of alternative opportunities to get her hands on it.'

Bea wondered what Clay and Lyon were taking about. The conversation in the far corner of the patio seemed to have run the gambit from the deeply morose to the nearly cheerful. Well, she'd find out later tonight when they were alone.

'I want to apologize,' Martha Herbert said to her.

'What?' Bea shifted her attention away from the men at the far end of the patio to Martha, who stood conspiratorially by her side. 'Apologize?'

'Do you remember the day that Morgan drove his RV over here to stay a few days? I stopped in to visit and found you both here on the patio talking. I think I jumped to a conclusion because I wanted to jump to a conclusion. It's hard for me to explain, but I knew that Rocco felt . . .'

Bea put her hand on the other woman's arm. 'It's forgotten, Martha. Really.'

Lyon realized that he stood at the parapet near the exact location where Rina had posed when she sensed the presence of her eagle. It was his turn to feel the bird's flight. High above them in the night the eagle soared a circling pattern. Rina was released and free.